Lois McMaster Bujold

This special signed edition is limited to 1250 numbered copies.

This is copy 1017 .

Masquerade in

LODI

Masquerade in LODI

A PENRIC & DESDEMONA
NOVELLA IN THE WORLD OF
THE FIVE GODS

Lois McMaster Bujold

SUBTERRANEAN PRESS 2021

First Hardcover Edition

ISBN
978-1-64524-047-1

Subterranean Press
PO Box 190106
Burton, MI 48519

subterraneanpress.com

Manufactured in the United States of America

*T*HE CURIA CLERK wiped the sweat drop from the tip of his nose before it could fall and blot his page. "What could be worse," he moaned, "than copying out letters in the Lodi midsummer?"

"Cutting up corpses in a Martensbridge midwinter," Penric replied unthinkingly, then pressed his lips closed.

The diligent if overheated clerk paused to stare. "What? You did that? …Was it for your magics?" He leaned slightly away, as if suspecting Penric and his resident demon of arcane midnight grave-robbery.

"Anatomy classes for the apprentices at the Mother's hospice," Pen clarified quickly. "Our material was donated by the pious, mainly." Plus the occasional unidentified, unclaimed body passed on by the city guard. The ones fished up from the thawing lake each spring had been the worst, if instructive.

"Oh. I did not know you'd been a medical student, too, Learned Penric."

I was teaching. Pen waved the comment away. This wasn't a topic he wished to pursue. Or a calling, but that conversation had been firmly concluded back in Martensbridge. The bulwark of a large mountain range now stood between him and his former failings, and he was grateful for it. The dead had not distressed him; the dying had. "It proved one task too many for my hands, and I gave it up."

A silent growl from Desdemona reminded him that self-castigation on this matter had also been firmly forbidden to him, under pain of demonic chiding. Since the bodiless demon that gave him the powers of a Temple sorcerer had been the successive possession of ten different women over two centuries before she'd fallen to Penric, she had chiding down to an art form.

Now, now.

Also nagging, he added.

Behave, or I'll blot your page as well.

Which, as a bored creature of chaos, she was well qualified to effect, in so many ways. His lip twitched, and, oddly cheered, he turned back to the last lines of his translation.

The clerk had a point. Six months ago back in Martensbridge, Pen would have had to burn expensive wood to warm his chambers this much, but the humid reek drifting in through the windows overlooking the canal made Lodi heat more oppressive, when no sea breeze relieved it. His own quill scratched as he converted the last lines of the letter from its original Wealdean into Adriac for the archdivine's eyes, and files, and handed it across to the clerk for copying.

This finished the morning's stack. Which contained nothing, it had proved, too sensitive or urgent. Done for the day, he trusted.

Busy work, sniffed Des. *Make-work. A waste of our talents.*

Speak for yourself. I find it soothing. Although he looked forward to an afternoon to devote to his own personal projects, including free run of the Temple library, far from fully explored in the four months of his residence in the curial palace. Penric cleaned his quill and stretched.

Tomorrow is the famous Lodi Bastard's Day festival, Des grumbled, *and you want to spend it shut up indoors? The preparations and parties are in full swing!*

So, people will all go out and leave me alone, Pen envisioned in hope. Although tomorrow night, he had social duties in the archdivine's entourage; the ceremonies dedicated to the fifth god were supposed to include a feast and a comic masque, and singing by the Temple-sworn castrati choir that was said to be ethereal. He anticipated that more warmly.

He sorted out those letters and their translations that actually required his superior's personal eyes, and with a cordial nod rose to leave the disposition of the rest to the very senior clerk, who wouldn't have wanted a demon of disorder anywhere near his files anyway. Pen wound his way through halls decorated with fine pious paintings and tapestries—or mostly pious; the previous generations of prelates had possessed a variety of tastes—and down a marble staircase to Archdivine Ogial's private cabinet.

The doorway was open to catch the nonexistent draft. Pen took it as invitation to rap on the jamb and put his head in. Gray-haired Ogial had surrendered his five-colored robes to the heat and hung them on a wall peg, and sat at his writing table in shirtsleeves. A lay dedicat in a grubby green tabard of the Mother's Order hovered anxiously at his elbow. The lad looked up and gulped as Ogial waved Penric inside.

"The Wealdean letters, Your Grace," Penric murmured, and laid them on the table.

"Ah. Thank you." The archdivine gave them a brief survey, then leaned back and looked at Pen with narrowing eyes. "What were your plans for the day, Learned Penric?"

Note past tense, Pen thought glumly, but mustered, "Any duties you assign, a bit more translation on Learned Ruchia's book, and then the library."

"Hah, I suspected as much." Ogial smiled with a paternal air, legacy of his early training in the Father's Order before he'd risen through the hierarchy to broader duties. "This is your first Bastard's Eve in Lodi, and you are a divine of His Order. You shouldn't miss it. Take the rest of the day off, get out of this musty curia, and see how our city honors your chosen god. But first..."

Saw that coming, murmured Des.

"Dedicat Tebi here brings me a request from the chief physician of the Gift of the Sea—the charity hospice for the sailors near the northwest harbor, you know—to send over a Temple sensitive to look at a poor mad fellow who was lately trawled up by some Lodi fishermen. One would think that being lost in the sea for, apparently, several days would be enough to turn anyone's brain, but Master Linatas says he finds something more than medically strange about this one."

Ogial picked up a note and twiddled it in his fingers in Penric's direction. Penric took it gingerly. The crisp writing didn't add much to the archdivine's precis, beyond the nameless patient's guessed age, early twenties, and coloration—caramel skin, curly dark hair, brown eyes—which described half the folk in Adria. The reported drooling, thrashing, and broken speech could denote, well, any number of conditions.

"You are well-fitted to sort out the medical from any uncanny diagnosis, I expect"—the archdivine raised a hand to stem Pen's opening protest—"in a purely advisory capacity, I promise. If the physician's more lurid concerns are misplaced, as such usually are, you can reassure him and be on your way at once."

True, mused Des, unruffled.

You just want the excuse to get out.

Likewise true. So?

Ogial turned to the dedicat. "Tebi, escort Learned Penric here back to your master, with my blessing upon your work. He's new to Lodi, so don't lose him in the back alleys or let him fall into a canal." He added to Penric with a chuckle, "Although if those whites of yours don't end up dunked at least once during the festival, you aren't doing the Bastard's Day right."

Pen managed an appropriate smile at the wit of his senior. And rescuer, he was reminded; the archdivine's prompt offer of employment in his curia had hooked Pen out of Martensbridge the moment the passes had cleared of snow in the spring. His half-bow grew more sincerely grateful. "Very well, Your Grace."

Tebi, dutifully preceding Penric out the door, cast a glance over his shoulder with scarcely lessened alarm. It couldn't be for Pen's vestments, an Adriac design common enough in so large a city—a close linen-white coat, fabric thin for the season, buttoned up the front to a high round collar and skirts open to the calves, handy to don over ordinary clothes. So, presumably, the unease was for the triple loop of braid pinned over Pen's left shoulder, the silver strand with the white and cream marking him as not just a regular divine, but a regulated sorcerer. If he did go out on the town tonight, Pen thought he might leave both items in his clothes chest, and not just for the hazard of the canals.

Pen attempted a friendly return nod, which didn't seem to reassure Tebi much. Pen wasn't averse to his garb buying him easy respect from adults, but he'd never expected it to frighten children. Or at least children schooled in the meanings of Temple trimmings.

We don't need the guide, Des opined as they exited a side door of the curia onto a non-liquid street. *I remember my way around Lodi well enough.*

From near a hundred years ago? Des's previous riders, the courtesan Mira and, come to think, her servant Umelan, had both been long-time residents of the town—then.

Islands don't move that much. Granted bridges rise and fall, and new buildings sprout—they detoured around just such a collection of scaffolding, stone, and shouting workmen—*but I could have landed us at the sailors' hospice all the same. I wonder if they still dub the place Sea Sick? Also, Learned Ruchia visited here more than once, on her assorted missions.* Des's immediate prior possessor, from whom Pen had so unexpectedly inherited the demon and her powers. And knowledge and skills. And opinions. And, yes, memories not his own. Pen wondered if that would ever stop feeling strange.

They angled through narrow shadowed streets and alongside translucent green canals, the margins of their enclosing pale stone walls stained dark by the rise and fall of tides. Their warm green scent permeated the air, distinctive but not unpleasant. The route led over five bridges, and through a couple of lively squares colorful with market hawkers, before the opening light and screeching of gulls marked them as coming out by the seaside.

Threading past bollards, quays, docks, a private shipyard—Pen could just glimpse the walls of the big state shipyard beyond, source of Lodi's famous war galleys—they turned into another street and square. A four-story building in warm gray stone flanked a whole side, and the lad led them through the thick wooden doors, one leaf propped open for the day. A porter rose from his stool, identified Tebi at a glance, and waved them on, though his gaze lingered curiously on Penric, who cast him a polite blessing in passing.

On the second floor, past the lair of an apothecary, Tebi knocked on the doorjamb of another writing cabinet: smaller, more cluttered, and less elegantly appointed than that of an archdivine. "Master Linatas?"

The man within turned in his chair, his leathery face animating at the sight of his messenger. He was a thick-bodied, muscular fellow, salt-and-pepper hair cut in an untidy crop, wearing a practical green smock shabby with wear and washings. The braids of a master physician hung not from his shoulder, but from a brass stand on his desk. "Good, you're back." A glance at Pen, and he lumbered to his feet. He still had to look up, his eyes widening slightly. "Goddess bless us."

Linatas could certainly read braids, so Pen merely said, "I'm Learned Penric. The curia sent me in answer to your request for a sensitive." Pen proffered the note by way of authentication.

Linatas took it back, still staring. "Huh! Are you, hm, Wealdean?"

A deduction from Pen's excessively blond queue and excessively blue eyes, Pen supposed, and his milk-pale scholar's skin. "No, I'm from the cantons."

"Ah, that would account for it. I've met merchants from those mountains, if not quite so, hm. Light. You speak Adriac very well!"

"I've a talent for languages, hence my employment in the curia."

The physician shrugged off Pen's appearance without further comment, thankfully, turning to his more pressing matter. "I suppose it would be fastest to just take you to the poor fellow. I've seen my share of men brought in with exposure, injuries, near-drownings, bad drink, or just too much horror, but this...ngh. Come this way. Ah, Tebi, thank you, well done. You can go back to Matron now." The boy nodded and scampered out. Pen followed Linatas up an end staircase to the next floor.

"Has anyone identified the man yet?" Pen asked.

"Not so far. Part of the time he talks like a Lodi man, but the rest is gibberish, crying, and these strange squeakings. He falls out of bed, staggers, writhes on the floor...we put him in a private chamber because he disturbed the other men in the ward so. Though since the fever from his parching has eased, it doesn't seem he's infected."

Pen bit his tongue on the impulse to run down the list of symptoms for strokes. He had only one task here, to assure the physician that his patient wasn't suffering from some unlikely curse, vastly more common in tale than in fact. And then he could escape. The familiar smell of a hospice, clean enough but distinctive, was making him just a little belly-sick.

Steady on, soothed Des.

I'm all right.

Uh-huh...

Linatas opened the door to a small chamber with a single cot. A harried-looking orderly was just thrusting a sunburnt young man back into it, who batted clumsily at him and whined.

Des, Sight. Pen stepped within; stopped short. The mystic doubled vision of his demon's view of the world filled his not-eyes. Mind, perhaps. *Oh.*

Bastard's tears, breathed Des. *There's a mess and a half.*

Within the sun-scorched fellow thrashed another demon. And not a new-hatched elemental, chaotic and weak, nor even one imprinted by some short-lived animal host. (And all animal hosts were short-lived, once an untutored demon of chaos infested them.) This was a demon of middling density, that had been human once, but then...

Des could read off its layers like the rings of a tree. *Elemental. Bird. Bird again. Human—a boy. Murdered, cruelly, young demon riven from him. Human, of no good character, but he didn't get away with his unholy theft for long. Roknari—they put him into the sea. For once, I can't object. Dolphin, quickly sickened. Demon dismasted of its acquired humanity, splintered, left a stub. Another dolphin, grieving—I did not know they could. Sickened again, more slowly. Then it found this fellow. So confused. The dying comforting the drowning… He thought he had gone mad when the demon jumped to him, and no wonder. Nightmare hours more in the water, then hands drawing him out, yes-no-yes-no…*

Pen wasn't sure which of them was shuddering. Well. Both, of course.

The young man stopped fighting, turned his head. Stared straight at Pen—and Des. He stiffened. Opened his mouth. And screamed and screamed. Because Sight cut both ways, when two sorcerers were thrown together.

Pen hastily backed out of the chamber and slammed the door. His shoulders found the opposite wall, and he fought for breath.

Even other Temple demons, tamed and trained, found Des's density frightening. Who knew what this wild thing made of her? Though as the screams trailed off Pen supposed he could imagine it. He was cursed with a much-too-vivid imagination, some days.

Most days, panted Des. *But now, I admit, it's justified.*

Linatas exited after him, eyes round with alarm. "Learned Penric! What is going on? You've turned absolutely green." He pursed his lips. "Which I'd always thought was a figure of speech—shock is more gray, usually. Must be an effect of your coloration."

Pen inhaled deeply. A couple of times. "You were right, Master Linatas. That's not any normal madness." Wait, was that a contradiction in terms? "Er, common madness. Your patient has contracted a demon. From a dolphin, or rather two dolphins. Who had it from a drowning Roknari, who stole it from a servant boy, who had it from, it seems, a couple of ordinary birds who'd scarcely altered the original formless elemental."

"You could tell all *that* from a glance?"

"No, from experience. Quite a lot of experience. You know how that works. Don't you." Pen managed an ironic eyebrow-lift. "Or you wouldn't have called me here, eh?" He straightened. "I don't know about your patient, but that demon is definitely insane."

Linatas was briefly speechless, taking this in. Had he really not expected validation of his half-formed suspicions? He found his footing in practicality. "What...should we do for him?"

"Certainly continue to keep him in isolation. That demon will be shedding disorder indiscriminately. Potentially dangerous to people and things around him. And to him." Penric winced an apology in prospect to Des. "It will have to be extracted from him by a dedicated saint of the white god."

This time, thought Des grimly, *no argument.*

Penric knew there was such a saint in Lodi, but not offhand at which of the scattered chapterhouses of his Order, or other domicile, said holy person might presently be found. It would seem easier to bring the saint here than the madman to the saint, but who knew. "I'll have to ask the archdivine, and make arrangements."

With a few moments to compose himself, Pen's mind was beginning to move again. Unfortunately into proliferating questions, like a dog scattering a flock of pigeons. "Did you speak to the men who brought him in? How long ago was that?"

"Briefly, and two nights ago. Ah, perhaps we should return to my cabinet and sit down for this." Linatas was still looking at his visitor with medical concern, though Pen was sure his color was coming back.

By the time they'd gone back downstairs, Linatas had parked Pen on a stool, pressed a beaker of tepid tea upon him, and watched to make sure he drank, the pigeons began to settle. Bird the first...

"Just where was he found, did they say?"

Linatas sat in his chair with an unhappy grunt. "About five leagues out to sea. Too far, really, to be a swimmer carried off by the currents. We guessed he must have been swept or fallen from the deck of a ship, although no returning vessel has so far reported a missing man."

"Was he a sailor, do you think?"

"No. He's very fit, or he wouldn't have survived his ordeal, but he doesn't have the hands of a laborer." Linatas held his up and clenched and unclenched them by way of illustration. "Deckmen's and fishermen's hands are very recognizable."

Working here for long, Linatas would surely have seen many such, right. "An officer? Seems too young."

"Lodi shipmasters apprentice young in their trade, but I think more likely he was a passenger."

Penric glanced down at his own writing callus and ink stains on his fingers. "Any sign of being a clerk or a scholar...?"

"Hm, not strongly marked, no. Perhaps a reluctant writer. When we can make out his speech, it's neither rude nor high." Linatas glanced at Pen with return curiosity. "Why did he scream so when he saw you?"

"Ah, not me. He saw my demon. Desdemona. Here, I'll lend her my mouth, and she can introduce herself. Des? Please be demure, now."

Des grinned; Pen could feel the set of his face change as she took charge. "Demure? Who do you think you're talking to? But I shall be properly polite, as befits a tame Temple servant. How do you do, Master Linatas? Thank you for looking after Pen, who tends not to do it for himself. Ah, perhaps that's demonstration enough, Des," Pen ended this before she decided it would be droll to embarrass him.

Spoilsport. But she settled back, gratified with her brief outing. And acknowledgment.

Linatas's thick eyebrows had climbed. "That... was not a jape. Was it?"

"No, though many people think it is." Pen sighed. "You may speak to her directly any time you wish. She hears everything I hear."

"...She? I mean, demons have no bodies."

"Very long story. About two centuries, so best not delay for it here. But getting back to your patient. Uh, how much do you know about Temple sorcerers? Or any sorcerers?"

"None have come my way as patients. I've seen them about town on rare occasions, or at ceremonies for their god."

Though if they were not in their whites and braids, Linatas could have passed such men and women unknowing in the market any number of times. For such a rare calling, the Lodi Temple was relatively well-supplied with sorcerers; Pen knew the Mother's Order here had more than one sorcerer-physician in its service, if not at this poorer hospice. Pen's duty directly to the archdivine was outside the usual chapterhouse hierarchy.

"At a minimum, I need to explain how ascendance works, then," said Pen. "As a creature of pure spirit, a demon requires a body of matter to support it in the world of matter. The question then becomes who shall be in charge of that body. A person can either possess or be possessed by their demon—rider or ridden is the usual metaphor—and demons in their untutored state naturally desire control. But as creatures of chaos, most aren't exactly fitted for it.

If a wild demon ascends, it's more like being taken over by a destructive, overexcited drunk." *With supernatural powers.*

You were doing all right till that last bit, Des said dryly.

"The other thing you need to know," Pen went on, ignoring the interpolation, "is that elementals, the bits of the Bastard's chaos leaked into the world, all begin as identical blank slates. Their ensuing personalities are acquired from and through their succession of hosts. *Imprinting* is a, hm, not-wrong way to envision it, like ink pressed down from a carved plate. Adding subsequent learning and life experience like any other person, but anyway. So every demon is different from every other demon just as every person is different from every other person, d'you see?" Pen looked up hopefully. This was a key point in his basic-demon-lecture where he often lost his listener to their prior more garbled beliefs. He'd also learned not to try to fit in all the fine points and exceptions at this stage, though the simplifications pained him.

Linatas gave him a *go-on* wave of his hand; if not exactly convinced, seeming willing to wait for it.

"Which brings us back to this demon." Unnamed, much as its possessor, or possessee. "It's very damaged. First, it came into being somewhere in the Roknari archipelago, which is, um, due to the Quadrene heresy not a healthy place for sorcerers or servants of the fifth god generally. The first animals it occupied were a couple of chance-encountered birds, nothing unusual there. But a demon, when its host dies, always tries to move up to a stronger—actually, more complex—host. The now-bird-imprinted spirit next went to a servant boy of maybe ten who, because Quadrene, would have known nothing about what was happening to him nor had any access to help or counsel. But someone else around him, a grown man, I think another servant, figured it out, and coveted what he imagined would be magical powers. Which, in his oppressed state, must have seemed worth the risk. He lured the boy out and secretly murdered him to steal those powers."

Linatas's head went back in surprise. "That's done?"

"It's tried. By the same sort of person who would commit murder and theft anywhere, I suppose. It...generally does not go as the assailant imagines it will." Pen cleared his throat. "His career as a would-be hedge sorcerer was evidently short, but long enough to attract the attention of the Roknari Temple authorities, who have rather different methods than us Quintarians to deal with problem demons. But effective enough in their way. He was put out to sea to drown. This prevents the demon from jumping to any other human. If no other large-enough creature is around in range to possess, the demon, um, well, *dies* is as good a term as any." *Evaporates* was another, but, fine points.

"Except this time, there *was* another creature, a curious dolphin. But when a demon is forced back to a lesser host, the effect on the demon's growing personhood is highly destructive. I've only seen one case where the demoted demon could be saved, afterward, and in that one the demon was unusually stable."

"*Save* a demon?" The *Whyever?* hung implied.

Des seemed a bit offended by the bafflement in Linatas's voice. Pen touched his shoulder braid, and put in on her behalf, "They give us great gifts, if they can be educated, and treated with understanding and respect. Like any other complicated thing of power and danger, which can kill you if misused. A water mill, a sailing ship, a hunting dog, a forge, a foundry—a human being. A pity and a waste when they are ruined."

Linatas, Pen had no doubt, had seen his share of pitiful waste in his line of work. By the twist of his lips, he was following the argument well enough for now.

"This demon seems to have been ruined twice over, once to be sure by its fall from human to animal, but more from its imprinting by the murdering servant. The apparent madness you are seeing in your patient is from moments of ascendance by aspects of this shattered demon. I suspect some of his gibberish is Roknari. I can't guess at the language of dolphins."

"That is the strangest part of all this, to me," said Linatas. "How he was saved by the dying dolphin, if that's what happened."

"Mm, maybe not so odd. Demons are the property, if you like, of the very god of chance and mischance. He looks after them, in His own way. The mark of His white hand seems all over this." And not for the first time, in Pen's experience.

"You're claiming a miracle?" Linatas's voice rose in pitch, as well as volume.

"In a sense. They say the gods are parsimonious, but I think a better term might be opportunistic. Your drowning patient doubtless prayed to any god listening for succor—I certainly would have, in his position—but the Bastard might merely have seen a good chance to recover His demon for proper disposal."

Now Pen was getting That Look, which he won so often when trying to explain his god's peculiar theology. He wasn't spinning fables, blast it. Or at least his was *informed* speculation.

"What I'm beginning to wonder more is how your fellow was parted from his ship in the first place. Since I don't imagine the god pushed him overboard. Not to mention who he is. Though once he is, ah, de-demoned by the saint, he should come back to his senses fairly quickly, and be able to tell us for himself what happened to him. So that's a set of problems that will solve themselves. The sooner, the better, I suppose."

Pen climbed to his feet. "I'll be back, or send a message. The demon will be struggling to stay on top, but it's possible your fellow may gain ascendance himself from time to time. You may be able to get more out of him then—he'll be speaking Adriac if he does. Probably." He wondered at the advisability of his next caution. It might cast an unfortunate doubt upon his own authority. Nevertheless. "Although demons can lie."

Lois McMaster Bujold

So can humans, muttered Des. *And rather more often.*

Linatas placed a hand on his desk preparatory to rising. "I'll call for Tebi to escort you back to the curia, Learned."

"No need. I know the way now."

"When will you return?" A tinge of anxiety colored Linatas's voice.

"Not sure. But I promise I won't delay. This has become the day's most urgent task."

Quick footsteps sounded from the hallway. A man in a green tabard whom Pen recognized as the orderly from upstairs stuck his head through the doorway, his gaze raking the room. "Not here," he muttered.

"Gnade?" said Linatas. "What's going on?"

"Sorry, sir. The madman got out when I went to empty the chamber pot. Only a moment—I'm sure he must still be in the building."

"Get Tebi to help you look."

"Right, sir." The orderly galloped off.

But Linatas did not relax back into his chair.

"Has your patient done this before?" asked Pen.

"He rattled around the ward obsessively yesterday, but he was pretty unsteady on his feet. He can't be far." Linatas's worried frown reflected no such certainly.

"Des?" said Pen aloud. "*Is* he still in the hospice?"

A dizzying roll of demonic perception stretched in three dimensions, dotted with the colorful glows of souls still in their bodies. Pen ignored the faint signatures of ghosts, gray and drifting and fading; all such old buildings had them, hospices more than most. The aura of the fractured demon would be a glittering beacon by comparison.

"No," said Desdemona through his mouth. Linatas glanced up sharply. "He's got out. That was fast."

Had Pen and Des triggered this very flight?

Likely, conceded Des. *The demon must have realized we're a danger to it, if not precisely how. That would depend on how much its hosts, past and present, understand Temple procedures. The mad Lodi boy may know more than the Roknari, and either would know more than the dolphins. Or the birds.*

An insane ascendant demon of disorder, loose in Lodi... The possibilities were daunting. Pen thought bad words in Wealdean.

Linatas pushed up from his desk.

"I'll help you look," sighed Pen.

THEY QUICKLY found from the porter that the run-away patient had not fled by the front door. Of the three other ground-level doors, two were locked from the inside. That narrowed the choice nicely. Pen, trailed by Linatas and Tebi, stepped out onto a side street and looked up and down. It would have been much too lucky for the man to still be in sight.

"If the demon is being dominated by the dolphins, it might actually try to get back to the sea. If by the one drowned and one near-drowned man, anything but." Pen bit his lip and pointed toward the harbor. "You two take that way. If he's jumped into the water, somebody should have seen him, this time of day. One of you could follow the shore in each direction. Look for a fuss. I'll head into town."

This logical plan was adopted without argument, seeming well to Pen till he came to the first cross-street. He halted in frustration.

"Des, if you were an insane demon, which way would you go?"

The sense of an offended sniff. *I am not insane. And I would do something much cleverer.*

Pen looked upward at the band of blue sky in vague futility.

This won a scoff outright. *As we have several times established, I can't fly, and neither can he.*

Might the distraught boy try to go home, wherever that was? *Would that demon be organized enough to pretend to be him? Well enough to fool people who know him?* It would be the most ready camouflage.

A doubtful pause. *It could submerge, let him take over and take them both home. But that would risk not being able to regain ascendancy.*

If the mad fellow was indeed a Lodi native, he would know this maze of a town. That knowledge would become increasingly available to the demon as it put down its roots into him, but not instantly. Pen remembered his confusion when he'd first contracted Des—more in the sense of a disease than a legal agreement, though there had certainly been negotiations later.

If, on the other hand, the demon was trying to get as far from the sea as possible, it, he, they had to head for the big causeway from the lagoon city to the mainland. The man had been bathed and shaved and fed in the hospice, but—how far could he bolt dressed only in a loose shirt and trews, barefoot and without money?

This was not getting them forward. He set his teeth and strode right, extending Des's perceptions to the limit of her range. Which was curtailed, in congested places like this, by the many distracting live souls around them. They came to another square where a canal intersected the street, small boats tied up supplying another busy local marketplace, loading and unloading: men, women, and children buying and selling bright vegetables, fruits, flowers, and more miscellaneous goods. The noise in his ears was merely cheerful. The glut in his Sight was near overwhelming.

Des, how can you bear it? All of us together?

A shrug. *I've never known anything else.*

There were good reasons why the very first thing Pen had sought, when this gift of Des's had come to him in full, was how to turn it off again. And it wasn't due to the poor sundered ghosts, much as they'd unnerved him back then. Nowadays, the worst part was when his trained brain started to *diagnose.* He really didn't want to know anymore which random strangers he met were dying.

All of them, eventually, Des observed.

I suppose in two centuries you've earned your long view.

The hard way, aye.

The Lodi madboy must be equally spirit-assaulted about now, if without the fine discernment Pen possessed. This suggested he might seek less peopled places, not that there were many in Lodi. Which pointed back to a break for the mainland, again.

Blast it, they needed to assign their quarry a name. Two names, as there were two agendas in play. He couldn't keep thinking of them as Lodi Madboy and Deranged Demon.

We could nickname them Mad and Dee, like Pen and Des, Des quipped. Pen rolled his eyes.

He circled the area, coming back to the front door of the hospice in time to meet Linatas and Tebi returning from their search of the shore. Alone.

At Pen's anxious look, Linatas shrugged. "No luck our way. Any from yours?"

Pen shook his head. "I covered about half of this island." After centuries of development, Lodi was still cut up into island-based neighborhoods, for all that some had been built out on pilings and dredgings to join up with each other. "Due to the demon, the problem of your patient has shifted from the Mother's Order onto the Bastard's." In other words, into Pen's lap. "He'll be leaking dangers far beyond his madness that can only be handled by a sorcerer or a saint. But please send his description at once to the causeway gate guards to be on watch for him." Which, given the fellow's common appearance, was going to be less than useful, but Pen could only work with what he had. "Tell them not to approach him, but to send a runner to..." Pen, ideally, but if he was out combing the city, he would be as hard to locate as his quarry. "Archdivine Ogial's office. Send there too if you learn anything more."

Which meant he needed to report in at the curia next, and warn them of their task as his message depot. Among other things.

Pen bade Linatas farewell with a cursory gesture of blessing, and hurried back over the five bridges. He made the return journey with his Sight at full stretch, just in case. It was like trying to rapidly skim a densely written book where paragraphs kept snagging and tripping his eye. The only thing he needed to discern of passersby was that they did not bear the demon, which was pretty instantly apparent. Unexpectedly exhausting; drawing Des's senses back in when he reached the curia, on the reasonable assumption that Madboy would not have come here, was a relief.

He scuffed up the stairs to the office on the second floor belonging to the archdivine's secretary, Master Bizond. At the doorway, he almost collided with a middle-aged woman in the trim black robe of the Father's Order. The black-and-gray braids of a full divine upon her shoulder were threaded with purple, marking a specialty in law. She carried a stack of papers and documents; reflexively, Pen held the door for her, which won him an abstracted nod of thanks. It inadvertently put her in line ahead of him at Bizond's desk.

Bizond was lean and gray and with the air of a permanent fixture in the curia, like the marble staircases. He looked up at the lawyer with something as close to approval as his stony features could unaccustomedly produce. "Learned Iserne."

The woman nodded crisply. "Here are the copies of the wills and documents for the Vindon lawsuit, together with my precis."

"Oh, good, we were waiting for those." His bony hands darted for them. A pause, while he sifted through in some preliminary assessment.

The woman, evidently feeling her mission discharged, eased back and eyed Pen in mild curiosity. "You are Learned Penric, are you not? Ogial's new sorcerer?"

Pen ducked his head. "Yes, Learned. I believe we have passed each other in the library?" He remembered her, dark-eyed and rather handsome for her age, hurrying in and out of the curial archives. Her glances at him had been neither impolite nor friendly; perhaps just distracted.

"Yes, I've noticed you." People typically did, with his height and eyes and hair. And braids. "Is it true you were court sorcerer to the princess-archdivine of Martensbridge?"

And now the subject of whispered curial gossip, Pen was dryly aware. "Formerly, till she sadly passed last year. The new royal appointee brought her own sorceress from Easthome, and I was encouraged to seek other employment."

Meaning, pressed hard to take formal oath at the Martensbridge Mother's Order as a full physician-sorcerer, in place of his unofficial service doing, actually, the same thing. But he wasn't discussing *that*. His sideways escape to Lodi had been unexpected even to him.

Pish, said Des. *Ogial leapt at your first note of inquiry. He considers you quite the ornament, you know.* The sense of a smirk. *Ornamental, too.*

The stack of documents was looking as if it might take some time. Shifting from foot to foot,

Pen blurted, "I'm sorry to interrupt, Master Bizond, but I have a bit of an emergency."

Bizond's face twitched from annoyance at this disruption of his concentration, to vague alarm at what a full-braid sorcerer of Pen's standing could possibly dub *a bit of an emergency*. His voice took a startled edge. "What?"

Swiftly, Pen gave the gist of his outing to the Gift of the Sea, minus the fine points. "The upshot is, if he hasn't made it across the causeway already, there is an ascendant demon loose in Lodi, riding, in effect, this kidnapped young man."

"This...is bad?"

"For the young man, yes. For whoever encounters him, I'm not clear yet. I will of course be going back out to look for him. Meanwhile, I need to know who and where is the saint of Lodi."

"Which one?"

"There's more than one?"

"Three petty saints that I know of in the Father's Order, and six scattered around the Mother's Order. I believe the Daughter's Order has a few as well. The Son's Order does not much run to saints."

"Er, I meant the one of my Order."

Bizond's eyebrows rose in surprise. "You don't know?"

Pen declined to explain how Lodi's demon-eating agent of the white god was someone Des would have preferred not to meet ever, settling on, "I'm new here...?"

"Ah, I suppose. Well, Blessed Chio may likely be found at the chapterhouse and orphanage on the Isle of Gulls. Do you know where that is?"

"Yes," Des replied for both of them.

Pen explained his plan to conscript Bizond's office for his message drop. Bizond, who had grown increasingly nonplussed through all this, didn't protest, though whether due to Pen's logic or his looming Pen wasn't sure. Pen hurried back out, trailed by Iserne's dazed stare and Bizond's mutter of "Five gods preserve us...!"

From the bedemoned boy? Pen wondered. *There is only one god for that task.*

I think he meant from you, said Des, too amused as usual.

As he left the curial palace again, Pen wondered whether it would be faster to walk or hail an oarboat. Des sketched a crude map in his head, and advised, *It will have to be a boat. Gulls is too far out for a bridge.*

Right. Pen switched directions to the boat-hire closest to the Temple square, at the edge of the city's central basin. Half-a-dozen narrow boats were pulled up at the dock, loading or offloading passengers: merchants and Temple folk and city officials. All the craft were painted and ornamented according to their owner-boatmen's tastes and notions of what might attract customers. The collective effect was clashingly gaudy: reds, oranges, yellows, greens, blues, some fresh, some weather-faded; stripes, swirls, solids, or carved animal motifs; polished tin or copper inlays glinting.

At the sight of his pale vestments and raised hand, a couple of the boatmen pretended to be looking the other way, but one aging fellow pushed back his hat, grinned, and waved Pen on. Pen stepped down carefully and centrally onto the damp, rocking planks and sank back on the worn cushion provided, which would have been more thoughtful for his lean haunches were it less compacted. He was still grateful to be off his feet for a bit.

"Bless us to avert your god's eye on His Eve, Learned, and where to?" the boatman inquired genially.

Pen dutifully returned a full tally of the gods, touching forehead, mouth, navel, groin, and heart, with a double tap of the back of his thumb to his lips. "The Isle of Gulls, please."

"Visiting the orphans?" The boat wobbled as the boatman pushed them off and out into the waters of the basin.

"The chapterhouse."

The boatman took up his stand at the square stern, and began to sweep his oar rhythmically back and forth in the squeaking oarlock. Progress was slow but steady, to the musical slapping of the choppy salt waves against the hull. Pen eyed the creaking seams beside his feet, but the tow and tar seemed to be holding, their sun-warmed odor evocative of marine livelihoods. *Keep your chaos to yourself, please, Des.*

Hah.

He gazed out across the basin, sparkling in this bright afternoon, sprinkled with other vessels of all sizes and sorts, moving or moored. A returning convoy of three big-bellied merchant cogs was the most impressive, as their happily shouting crews warped them in to their anchorages, canvas thumping down. Pen would have enjoyed the sight more if he'd been less distracted. Des felt uneasy within him as they bobbed across the waves, like incipient seasickness.

You've been involved in such demon-retrievals more than once before, haven't you, in your career as a

Temple demon? Part inquiry, part reassurance. *Poor Learned Tigney, I know about. His affair wasn't that much before my time.*

Agh, yes. That idiot. He preened so when he was first gifted with his demon by the Order, certain he would soon surpass Ruchia and me. We weren't in Martensbridge when his demon ascended and absconded, but we were saddled with the task of tracking them down when we got home. He led us a vile chase across Trigonie. We only caught up with him because he'd stopped too long in a town just over the border of Orbas to pursue an excessive course of carnal pleasures.

The way demons do, Pen put in slyly. When they had the chance, in their stolen, or shared, carnal bodies. Though after ten years together, he was over his embarrassment by Des's enjoyment of his. Mostly.

And men do, Des shot back. *When both surrender to one desire, there are no brakes. If I were not much more balanced,* she continued primly, *I could not have lasted this long. Howsoever, Tigney's demon seemed more addicted to gluttony and sloth than, say, lust and wrath, which fortunately slowed them. Though the pride and envy by which he first fell was all Tigney.*

Pen mused on her list. *So where does greed fit in all this?*

Just middling. Greed is an appetite that looks largely to some imagined or feared future. Ascendant demons are not much known for foresight.

Hm. Pen frowned as they approached the boat landing on the island shore. *So did you bring the saint to Tigney, or him to the saint? It was still old Blessed Broylin of Idau back then, wasn't it?* A creaky and cranky old man when Pen had so memorably met him, until the god had shone through his eyes like a dive into infinite space.

Fifteen years ago, so not as creaky. Though just as cranky. We dragged Tigney back to him.

We need to discuss the mechanics of that.

Less mechanics than force and threat. Ruchia's guards supplied the force; she and I supplied the threat.

Will you be able to overawe this wild demon?

...Probably.

Only probably? Pen didn't quite like that hint of doubt. *It must surely be less powerful than Tigney's was.*

Lack of foresight, remember. Fear can be the opposite of greed, that way, shortening one's horizon.

I'd have thought Tigney's demon would have been utterly terrified, knowing exactly what was in store for it.

When terror surpasses all bearing, it can tip over into despair. And a sort of docile lassitude.

A relief of sorts?

Not really.

"You're a quiet one," remarked the boatman as he steered them to their island docking.

Not on the inside of my head. "Sorry. I've a few things on my mind."

The boatman's eyebrows twitched up at the apology. "Busy night coming up for you folks of the fifth god, with the festival and all?"

"I expect so." Though not, in his case, due to the festival.

The boatman chortled. "Don't celebrate so good you dunk that white dress in a canal."

What is this obsession by everyone we meet with my whites and canals?

Des would have smirked if she could. As it was, Pen's lips twitched. *Hopeful anticipation, probably.*

They glided into perfect position at the algae-fringed stone quay. Heartened by his customer's near-smile, the boatman added, "D'you want me to wait for you, Learned?" He named the fee for this restful service as Pen drew up his purse on the cord around his neck and fished out the right coin.

He'd been relieved, like most Lodi visitors, that boatmen's rates were set by law and posted on all public landings.

"I'm not sure how long I'll be here." He considered Madboy, who-knew-where doing who-knew-what by now. "But I won't be lingering. Yes, please." He added the half-in-advance coin to the boatman's outstretched leathery palm, and turned to climb the steps.

More remote than its sister city wards, the Isle of Gulls was less built-up, the households scattered across it sparing space for gardens and orchards and useful domestic animals. It gave the place a restful, rural air that Pen discovered he'd missed in the scurry of the Temple precincts in Lodi's heart. The chapterhouse of the Bastard's Order was not hard to find, as a channel was dug from the shore near the landing right up to its walls, and through a water gate presently raised.

When this place was a merchant's mansion, Des reminisced, *he passed his goods in and out that way. When he died childless, he left house and fortune to the Order to build on the orphanage. That was back in Mira's day. We knew it well then, as we'd come out here for patrons on occasion. Mira had the most flamboyant boat, with an awning of silk and liveried oarsmen.* A nostalgic sigh. *It's changed...* A century had softened the raw brick; the walls were climbed now by no enemy more dangerous than ivy.

A high wooden gate stood half open to the afternoon, cheery voices floating through it. Pen entered to find two boats pulled up from the terminating pool of the small channel. A motley assortment of children laughed and argued around them, engaged in decorating wherever decorations could be fitted on, ribbons and bannerets and garlands of miscellaneously colored cloth flowers clearly made by little hands. They were benignly supervised by a pair of adults in stained white dedicat's tabards, who looked up in question at Pen's arrival.

"May I help you, sir?" said the man.

Pen supposed he'd better go through proper channels. How did one gain audience with a saint? Should he have tried to send ahead for an appointment? "I'm Learned Penric of the archdivine's curia. I need to speak with the head of the chapterhouse."

"Of course, Learned. Please come this way." With a cautious and deeply curious glance at Pen's left shoulder, the man led off across the trampled yard toward the stately house, two stories high and faced with fine creamy stone, window frames and doors painted russet. "Oh, there he is now."

A distracted-looking man in bleached vestments cut much like Pen's, if more worn and less ink-spattered around the cuffs, and with the badge of his office hanging from a silver chain around his neck, exited the front door and looked around. He spotted Pen at once, his brows drawing together. Pen pegged him for another middle-aged functionary, more administrator than holy man, the backbone of every Order.

They met at the foot of the shallow steps. The dedicat bobbed his head. "Learned Riesta, this is Learned Penric. He says he's come from the curia."

"Oh," said Riesta. His tone seemed more enlightenment than surprise.

"Pardon me for arriving unheralded," Pen began politely, "but I seek an urgent conference with the saint of Lodi, whom I was told resides here."

"Yes, that's right." He continued to peer perplexed at Penric. "Is there something the matter with your Temple demon, Learned Penric?"

"Not at all," Pen assured him hastily, while Des puffed in silent offense. "I was detailed by the archdivine"—yes, given Pen's own deceptively unweathered features, it never hurt to prop his authority—"to deal with another matter, which is going to require the blessed one's attention. Uh, I trust the saint is here?"

"Yes. Blessed Chio awaits you in the garden. I was told to bring you around." Waving his dedicat back to his orphan-supervising, Riesta led off along the flagstone walkway bordering the old mansion.

"The saint knew I was coming?" Disturbingly possible, in the god-touched.

"It seems so," sighed the chapter head, in an oddly put-upon tone. "This was only announced to me a few minutes ago."

The garden might once have been formal, but was given over now to more practical vegetables and fruit trees, tidy as a stitched sampler. A dedicat and a couple of what were probably more orphans knelt weeding on the far side. The only other occupant sat on a bench under an old peach tree, its branches bending with still-green fruit. It was a young woman, barely more than a girl. Her thin white coat, unadorned by any sign of rank, was worn carelessly open over an ordinary faded blue dress. Pen blinked, startled.

You shouldn't be, said Des. *A saint can be anyone at all, you know that. Anyone whose soul gives space for a god to reach into the world. ...Not sorcerers, naturally.*

The god was not immanent now, or Des would be reacting more violently. As they trod up, Pen studied Chio's exterior appearance.

Dark hair in a simple braid down her back, finished with a white ribbon. Skin a typical Adriac honey. Amber-brown eyes, well-set in a long narrow face with rather a lot of chin and nose. In middle age, her features might still be dubbed handsome, if she were fortunate in her health; in sunken old age, possibly a little scary, but in the flower of youth they remained memorably pleasant. Pen wasn't sure whether to revise her estimated age upward at her well-filled bodice.

No telling, said Des. *Some of us started early—Mira was one. Vasia was another.* She left off, thankfully, without detailing ten different examples of female puberty.

Chio looked up at him with equal attention. "Oh," she said, in a voice of surprise. "You're not quite what I was expecting."

The feeling is mutual. Pen didn't think her narrowing eyes expressed disappointment, but what she was making of him was not obvious.

Riesta performed a brief introduction, ending with, "What's this all about, Learned Penric?"

Pen scratched his ear, marshaled his story, again. Having explained it once already today helped, but Pen suspected Chio's was a very different listening from Bizond's. He didn't need to recap basic demon lore here, but...she couldn't possess Idau's long years of experience, surely.

It's not the saint's experience that matters. It's the god's, said Des. *I don't think we need worry about that part.*

Finishing his tale of the shiplost lad, Pen settled on a tentative, "Have you had to do yet with removing a dangerous demon from a person?"

She shrugged one slim shoulder. "It's mostly been fetching out young elementals from animals. That's how the god first came to me, four years ago—one of the householders on the island thought her cow was sick. Which it would have become, shortly. She was most pleased when I seemed to cure it. A Temple sensitive soon brought me an infested cat, my power was proved—I could have told them so, but who listens to a fourteen-year-old girl? A fuss followed, and then a further parade, well, trickle of elementals, and here I am. Still."

Riesta listened to this with a rather fixed smile.

Chio brightened. "I did get to go to the mainland one time, for a woman who'd caught an elemental from one of her chickens. And once for a horse."

Pen tried not to let his mind be diverted by the picture of a demonic chicken. Des's sojourn in the world had begun with a wild hill mare and a lioness, after all.

I wonder if that woman ate the chicken, as the lioness did the mare? Des mused.

She'd no doubt started out to slaughter it for her table. It would have been a short and enticing, if ultimately unlucky, jump for the demon. Also, how would you tell with a cat...? *Never mind.*

Pen was reminded of the old saw about the recipe for rabbit stew. *First we catch the demon.* "It's my belief that the ascendant demon is still hiding somewhere in Lodi. My next task is to find him. When I accomplish that, I'll wrestle him out here to you." Against the demon's uttermost resistance, no doubt, but Pen would cross that bridge, or boat ride, later. "But I thought I'd best meet and warn you, first. I'm, um, not actually sure how long this retrieval will take, but I trust you will be here?"

She studied him back with disquieting intensity. "No..." she said slowly. "I think it will be better if I go with you." Her eyes glinted as she straightened. "Yesss...perfect."

Riesta choked. "Blessed, surely not. Town will be riotous tonight. You know you are safer here."

"I'd think the archdivine's own court sorcerer would be worth a dozen guardsmen, don't you?" Her smile seemed a sly challenge: *Deny that, if you dare.*

Pen wondered why Des was suddenly amused.

Chio bounced to her feet. "There, that's settled. I'll just go get my things."

There had been no discussion at all. For one thing, no one had asked *him* if he wanted to take on the escort of this young woman. Saint. *God-vessel.* On the other hand...if she were with him when he found Madboy, the god's demon-removal could be performed at once, saving a great many hazardous steps. Hm...

Riesta, watching her swiftly receding back, sank to the bench with an *oof.* Pen perched beside him.

"Did the god just speak through her?" Riesta asked Pen plaintively.

No? Yes? "Our god speaks in mysterious ways. Usually maddening riddles, to be frank. So I'd hesitate to say no."

"She *knows* that, you realize." Riesta vented a sigh. "It's not that she's not god-touched. It's not even that she's not all there, but that she's not all... here. Sometimes. And at others she's a trammeled and difficult young woman much like any other her age. The trouble is, I'm never sure which one I'm talking to, or is talking to me. When she figured that out, I was never in control again, yet I remained in responsibility."

Pen offered a sympathetic nod. "Did she grow up here in your orphanage?"

"Yes, she was a foundling. Probably bestowed at our gate by one of Lodi's prostitutes. We get a steady supply of such. She seemed an ordinary enough girl, on the quiet side, just fair in her studies—she was supposed to have been apprenticed to a dressmaker, was about to leave us, but then this other thing happened."

"Not the apprenticeship you expected, I take it?"

"Nor anyone else. After the archdivine inspected her, we were ordered to keep her here and give her theological instruction, and hold her at the disposal of the Temple. This...has not always gone well."

It finally dawned on Pen that the man's anxiety was not for Chio, but for him. Trying to delicately warn that this girl would lead her escort by the nose if she could, without actually saying anything rude about his saint? Penric considered Des's two centuries of female experience. *Think you can handle her, Des?*

The girl, yes. The saint... At least, unlike Riesta here, I will be able to tell which one is talking.

"I think it will be all right," said Pen, more out of hope than experience. "The god wants His demon back. Through her, He may even be able to help speed my search."

"No doubt the god will protect her." Riesta didn't sound all that confident.

With reason. However god-touched, saints were ultimately human beings, frail flesh like any other person. Without which, Pen was reminded, the gods could not reach into the world at all. *The gods do not save us from death. They only catch us when we fall from life.* Pen also translated that as, *Don't lose my saint in a canal!* Fair enough.

A tabarded dedicat ventured up, ostensibly to ask her superior some question about arrangements for tomorrow's festivities; more, Pen suspected, to get a closer peek at the mysterious visitor from the curia. Riesta sent her off for tea. It was served cool and sweetened with honey, along with a plate of grapes, cheese, and bread, for which Pen realized he was ravenously grateful—lunch had been mislaid somewhere in his day's travels.

By the time this refreshment was consumed, they were still waiting for Chio. Pen hoped his boatman was faithful. Although if the fellow had given up and poled off, Pen supposed there would be another one along. The basin was busy this time of day.

At last the saint tripped back, looking suspiciously satisfied with herself. Her braid had been wound up and secured on the back of her head with some fetching hair sticks, cut-glass balls on their ends glittering as she moved. Her white coat was buttoned up to her throat, though a different skirt hem fluttered at her ankles. A lumpy linen bag swung from her hand. Pen eyed it in some bafflement.

"Let's go, then!" she declared.

Pen was willing, though beginning to wonder what they would do when they reached the city shore. He needed a better plan than randomly, or even systematically, continuing to quarter Lodi with his uncanny sense being battered by every soul in it but the one he sought. With old Idau in his mind as the model for a saint, he supposed he'd been vaguely counting on some sage, avuncular advice here at the chapterhouse to direct his steps further. Though if he'd wanted to be led, he now had it—Chio grabbed Pen's hand to drag him off. She walked backward a moment to wave a cheerful farewell to the glum Riesta, who called parental-sounding cautions after her as they made their way around the old mansion.

They were delayed at the gate by an ambush from the children, who demanded Chio inspect and approve their boat-decorating. Pen, taking his cue from her, strove to come up with a few admiring comments as well. It was plain Chio's words were more treasured.

She smiled over her shoulder as they left the walls of the chapterhouse compound. "I used to do that, help decorate the boats every Bastard's Day."

"To be part of the ceremonies tomorrow, I take it?" At her puzzled glance up at him, he added, "I only just arrived in Lodi a few months ago."

"Oh. Yes. All the chapterhouses and orphanages have a boat parade around the canals in honor of the god. Isn't your chapterhouse...?"

"I work directly for the curia, so no."

"The archdivine does come out and bless us at the start."

"Boat races, too?"

An amused smirk, which looked well on her lips. He was beginning to suspect the girl hid more wits than she displayed. "Of course."

Of course. As far as Pen could tell, there was no event in Lodi that was not considered pretext for the population to show off their boats and boat-prowess to each other. High holy days. Low holy days. Weddings. Funerals. Ship-launchings. Guild anniversaries. High appointments in the ducal court or the archdivine's curia. Pen understood that the oarboat races among the more athletic ladies of the bordellos on his god's day were particularly popular with the spectators.

"I was let to ride in the chapterhouse parade twice, when I was younger," Chio went on. "All the children chosen to go get wildly excited about it. If we made ourselves look especially well and clean, we all imagined that someone in the crowd would pick us to go home with them as apprentice or even, highest prize, adoptee. Which did happen sometimes, though not to me." Her smile turned wry. "I was horribly disappointed. But then a better Adopter found me, and I was glad for my sadness in hindsight."

The faintly defiant way her chin rose made Pen wonder if this last statement was quite true.

As they came to the landing, where Pen was relieved to find his boatman still reclining under his broad-brimmed hat, she suddenly asked, "Do you have much money?"

"Er, the archdivine pays me a generous stipend?"

"I mean *on* you."

"Oh. Enough, I suppose. Should I encounter an unexpected expense, I could return to my chambers for more." He wondered if his vestments and braids and high employment would buy him trust for temporary credit. With his tranquil life inside the curia, it wasn't a problem he'd needed to test, yet.

"That's all right, then." She gave a sharp, satisfied nod, making her hair ornaments splinter tiny rainbows.

Unfolding from his paid repose, the boatman tried to not look too amused at Pen's sudden acquisition of a young lady on his arm; their garb hinting, correctly as it happened, at some mutual Temple business. The man handed her down into the boat with no more banter than a few helpful directions. They found their balance and started off again across the basin. The slanting sun painted the busy waters with shimmering liquid gold.

Pen's appreciation of the beauty of the light was undercut by his unease at time getting away from him. Where in Lodi might the deranged demon choose to hide his ridden partner? In some obscure corner? Or in the holy eve crowds, which were going to be out in force tonight?

He turned back to find Chio unbuttoning her pale coat. The dress revealed beneath was much lower-cut across the bodice than the demure maiden's pale blue she'd been wearing earlier, set about with bits of lace and ribbon, and woven in sophisticated dark blue and cream vertical stripes. In fair condition but not new—orphanages often acquired overfine if damaged garments from the wardrobes of wealthy women patrons. Pen wondered if she'd mended it with her own needle, and if she regretted her lost chance at becoming a dressmaker.

She folded the coat and stuffed it into the sack, exchanging it for a holiday half-mask in silk decorated with sequins, a fringe of white and blue feathers lending it visual clout. She held it up to her eyes and grinned at Pen under it. It turned her visage mysterious, older. How alarmed should he be with this transformation? Des remained merely amused, though, so maybe it was all right?

"I was going to wear this dress for my birthday tomorrow," she answered whatever taken-aback look Pen was sporting. The mask came down, and the usual Chio returned. "But if we're off to the Bastard's Eve, I thought I'd start tonight."

"Your birthday is on our god's day? That's supposed to be lucky." Which flavor of luck, good or bad, usually left unspoken.

She shrugged. "It's not that special. All the foundlings who arrive around midsummer without any other identification get assigned the Bastard's Day as their birthday. We always got sweet custards at dinner together anyway."

"Ah," Pen managed.

THEY ARRIVED back at the Temple precincts' boat landing with Penric no more inspired as to his next move. As he helped Chio up the steps, Pen asked, "Does our god give you any clues how we should shape our search?"

She shook her head. "Nothing yet."

Pen was unsurprised; if the god had so much as whispered to her, Des would have reacted, strongly. This was still only Orphan Chio, not Blessed Chio.

"I'd better check in at the curia first, in case any messages have arrived." It was, he supposed, entirely too optimistic to hope for news that their quarry had been captured and was being held for them by the causeway guards.

Ordinary guards could not restrain him, Des noted.

Pen wasn't sure how able that demon and its confused, ridden host would be to fight armed men—Des could make short work of such opponents, if they were not too many—but it had been adept enough to readily escape the hospice. Best not underestimate. Worse, the demon might be careless of the life of its mount, since it could just jump to another host if poor Madboy were, say, run through with a sword. *Ngh.*

Offering his arm to Chio, which she took with a small smile, he chose a different route back to the curia building, his Sight again extended. He realized his mistake as they circled through the main city square, which would take them past the gibbet. To his relief, it was empty, no raucous crowd around it being more entertained than edified by the price of crime.

Nor would it be used tomorrow. There were no executions on the Bastard's Day: not in reprieve for the condemned, but to grant holiday to the hangmen, one of the many questionable callings that came under the fifth god's cloak. And, in theory, under Pen's care as a seminary-trained divine, but such pastoral duties usually fell to more regular servants of his Order. If they weren't sundered into dwindling ghosts, the souls the executioners sped might go to any god at all, to the frequent confusion of the onlookers.

Ordinary living folk hurrying across the square to duties or dinner pressed upon him hard enough. Chio looked up shrewdly at him, and asked, "Does your Sight hurt you, Learnèd?"

"Um..." He didn't want to admit *Yes* to her. "It's a strain, but bearable." It would be a lot more bearable were it rewarded with some results, but he felt nothing more than too-complicated humanity all the way to the curia doors.

Chio's bright soul could not be the least complex of these, but Des's Sight seemed to slide around her.

Is the god keeping you out?

No, she said shortly. *Would you walk on the edge of a precipice?*

Yes, if I wanted to see over.

Ugh. You canton mountaineers and your heights.

Des's aversion to altitude had been hard-earned, so Pen didn't quibble with her metaphor. Demons were more durable than humans in their fashion, and Pen had become all too familiar with Des's fearlessness, but perhaps the absence of risk should not be mistaken for the presence of fortitude.

Don't be rude. You have your own sources of helpless terror. A thoughtful pause. *In your case, frequently moral rather than mortal, but deadly all the same. Scars on your arms faded yet?*

Yes. Thank you. And my apologies.

That's better.

The ornate colonnade of the curia was flushed dusky pink in the fading light. At Bizond's chamber, they found the senior secretary gone home for the day, his place taken by a night clerk.

"So you are why I'm here," the man sighed, sounding not best pleased to be missing the holiday eve, if resigned. But there were no messages yet. It was too soon to mutter frustrated curses in Wealdean, though Pen was tempted. Chio seized the chance to leave her sack with this trustworthy guardian.

They came back out on the Temple square after a short detour for the saint to inspect the sculptures that graced the main entry, not a little of it war booty.

Pen wondered at a world that hanged poor men for thievery, but celebrated great ones.

"Now what?" said Chio, looking around at the growing shadows muted by a still-luminous sky.

Pen rubbed his face, mulling. "Go back to the beginning and start over, I think. To the Gift of the Sea. It would at least put one certain end of the trail in my hand. And Master Linatas might have heard something more." After the threat from Penric and Des had cleared out, could the demon even have slipped back to the place it had been fed and cared for? It seemed unlikely straw-clutching.

Pen chose a different way back to the farther shore of town, which involved seven bridges, not five, and took them down a few darkened alleys that would have been more daunting were Des not the most dangerous thing in them. The paths alongside the canals were better lit, partly by lanterns bobbing along raised up on the sterns of the oarboats busy with transporting holiday-goers in fancy dresses and masks. Laughter as well as light rippled in their wake across the night-silk waters.

With full dark, the more restrained parties had withdrawn indoors to the wealthier houses. *Also the more randy ones,* Des put in. *Mira did so enjoy those, in her day.* Music drifted down from radiant upper windows overlooking the canal paths. But a few canal-side markets had been given over to neighborhood celebrations, young and old combining to set up trestle tables for foodstuffs and booths from local taverns. It was still early enough in the evening that most of the shrieking came from running, overexcited children, but several tables sent up volunteer choruses of hymns, drinking songs, and, at the more inebriated, parodic combinations of the two. The cleverest made Pen grin.

"Oh, gorgeous, grant me a godly kiss from that *mouth*," came a drunken cry from offside. Pen wheeled, preparing to fend off a happy-sounding assault on the saint. Which was how the fellow managed to fall on *him.* Pen dodged fruity wine-breath—this one must have started celebrating well before sundown, the official start of the Bastard's Eve. He gritted his teeth and used the fellow's stumbling momentum to forward him into the nearby canal, where he fell with a mighty splash. His companions, equally drunk but not so amorous, laughed uproariously and lurched to fish him back out.

"Good work, Learned!" one cried in passing, attempting to congratulate him with a shoulder-bump.

Pen dodged that, too. He grasped Chio's elbow and drew her back through the crowded square to the less hazardous building-side, sparing a glance to be sure the idiot was retrieved. Some Lodi canals could be waded across, but others were ten, twenty, or more feet deep, and swallowed the careless with tragic consequences. It looked like this was going to remain a comedy.

Chio, at least, was amused, her amber eyes glinting in the lantern light. "Does that happen to you often, Learned Penric?"

"*All the bloody time*," Pen answered, goaded. He brushed down his coat, which was growing too warm as the humid night failed to cool, and tamped his temper. "It's not worth my effort to get offended. Although I am sometimes put to it when some, er, suitor takes his rejection in bad part. That can get dangerous."

"For you?"

"For him." Or her, but peeved females did not usually resort to physical violence. Poisonous words he could endure.

It was her turn to murmur, "I see," concealing private thoughts. One escaped: "Do your suitors ever succeed?"

"Not that sort." Pen sighed. "And the quiet, bookish types I might actually enjoy talking with are too shy to ask, leaving me only with the others."

She looked around, straightened brightly, and dragged him to a nearby booth. "Here's a solution. Because we wouldn't want more delay tonight. Buy yourself one."

It boasted a display of holiday masks in a multitude of designs, from cheap and plain to much less cheap. Had that been a saintly order? Or did the girl just want her escort to look more the part of half a couple?

Under the benign gaze of the booth's proprietress, Pen reached for the plainest linen half-mask on the rack. Chio's hand caught his wrist.

"No," she said in a thoughtful tone, "I think this one would suit you better." She handed him a mask molded in the shape of a stern white lion, subtly made and convincing, its price reflecting its art.

Pen knew he'd not told her about the lioness that made up that long-buried layer of his demon. Was this coincidence, or something more unsettling?

In any case he dutifully acquired the mask, to Chio's obvious approval. "Good," she said. "You look more imposing now. There's still the unfair jaw and mouth, but this should deter all but your worst admirers."

He did not escape the square before also purchasing at her demand a posy of fresh white flowers shaped in a bracelet for her slim wrist, stewed meat wrapped in thin pancakes, and candied fruit on sticks. At least they could eat the latter as they walked.

He kept his senses extended as they continued along the canal, sieving the flux of passing souls: on the path, on the waterway, tucked up in the surrounding houses. So many, so heaped. So not-demonic. Searching, walking, eating, and talking all together was very distracting. He kept as far from the bank as he could while still sheltering Chio on his other side.

"Do you have any money?" he thought to ask Chio in turn. "On you, I mean." Should they get separated, she should at least have the price of an oarboat back to the Isle of Gulls. Though if any oarsman would accept her promise, he supposed someone at the chapterhouse would settle up on her arrival.

"Of course not," she said. "The chapterhouse covers all my keep. And my travels, should I have any."

"Doesn't the Temple pay you a stipend?"

"Me?"

"It should. Blessed Broylin of Idau is paid one, I know." Through a different realm's Temple administration, but still.

"Really!" A glance up, then a thoughtful hum. "Do you know how much?"

"Not offhand. He's a retired baker, I believe, so has some money of his own. Any chapterhouse that wants him to travel pays his way, of course, but the stipend is separate. I don't know if it's his age or his calling that makes him uninterested in riches, but he's kept decently."

"I had no idea saints could be *paid*."

"You are, in your way, Temple functionaries, the same as divines or sorcerers." *Well…not* quite *the same*, murmured Des. "Your soul may belong to our god, but your body is owed any body's wage."

"No one has ever suggested that before." Her lips pursed in, Pen feared, calculation.

Are we creating chaos, Des?

This one is all your doing, Pen. A pause. *I approve, of course.*

Chio's mask tilted toward him in new curiosity. "Have you had your demon long, Learned Penric?"

"Since age nineteen."

"Huh! That's just a year older than I am now."

"So it was." Had he really been that young?

Yes, sighed Des.

"Ten years ago, now. Odd. It seems longer. A third of my life." And four years a saint made almost a quarter of Chio's short life. He asked in return interest, "Was it lonely for you in the orphanage? After your calling came upon you?"

Her mouth rounded in bemusement, as if no one had asked her that question before. "It was different. My old friends fell off, though everyone was scattering to their apprenticeships by then anyway. Except for Carpa, who is going to be five years old and there forever, poor girl. But the divines swarmed me. They made me read piles of theology, and I am not bookish. Teaching the orphans to sew or cook is far more fun." She added politely, "No offense to you, Learned Penric."

"None taken. I admit some of those tomes can get, er, turgid."

"Yes, and that's so *wrong*." She made a face. "I could tell, after a while, which writers *knew* and which ones were reciting by rote. The divines didn't like it when I told them so."

Pen grinned. "I imagine not."

"Do they have the saying in Wealdean about locking the stable door after the horse is stolen?"

"In just those words, yes."

"It was like that. The divines and all those books."

He sobered, remembering that visceral, direct experience of the unimaginably vast that defeated all words. Young, guarded from the world, not bookish, all these Chio might be, but in certain dimensions profoundly not ignorant. "I've told the tale of how I acquired Desdemona at the death of Learned Ruchia so many times, it might as well be a rote recital by now. But when I try to describe what happened with Blessed Broylin..."

She smiled into his lengthening silence. "Yes. Exactly that."

They turned the next corner into a narrower street. No canal here, but Pen linked her arm through his to prevent stumbles in the dark. The lack of animal traffic made Lodi streets cleaner than those of inland towns, and the tide carried off most of the rest of the residents' refuse, but not, alas, all.

"Is it lonely being a sorcerer?" she asked abruptly.

"No, because I'm never alone." Reflecting on his past decade of nesting in narrow chambers in other people's palaces, he rethought this. "Although I'm never sure if people are taking my braids as a mark of rank or a plague warning."

She snickered. "I've not actually talked much to the sorcerers, despite my calling. They bring me the elementals and then leave as soon as possible."

He thought of the city gibbet they'd lately passed. "Desdemona once told me it's like watching an execution. For a demon. So I'm not greatly surprised."

"Your demon seems calmer than most."

"We've been through something like this before. Me once, Des two centuries' worth."

She nodded. "Dispatching elementals for the Order had started to feel more like killing chickens for the god's kitchen than anything holy, even leaving out that real chicken. But then there was the horse. Speaking of horses."

"Hypothetical absent horses. I take it this was a real one?"

She waved her free hand in sudden delight. "It was the first demon the god refused to take from me. It was a very good horse, so beloved, trained for parades and for children to ride. And beautiful! The glossiest beast I ever saw. The god sent it back to be raised as a Temple demon, to go to some learned sorcerer-candidate next. Its family was very relieved to be told it could live out its life with them."

"That was remarkably kind of the Order. And wise."

"Your demon must know of this. She's stood at the gate of her riders' deaths for such judgment and been told to go back, what, twelve times you said?"

Pen hadn't said. "That's right." After so many passages, did it feel to Des as if that gate was narrowing upon her?

Yes, she muttered.

Pensive, Chio went on, "I'd always felt the god's sorrow, before, when I did His work. Never His joy. I finally knew what I was here for. I keep hoping for another one like that lovely horse."

"The Order does, too," said Penric. "Though I'm afraid this mad boy's demon isn't going to be one."

No, agreed Des grimly.

The vague scent of canal sewage gave way to a more estuarial tang as they came out at the big northwest harbor. Not many lights here; should he have acquired a linkboy's lantern at the marketplace?

"Can you see in the dark, as sorcerers do?" he thought to ask Chio.

She shook her head. "I see the same as everyone else. Until the god is upon me, and then I see everything. Whether I want to or not."

"Ah."

Helpfully, a bright lamp over the main entry of the hospice guided them in.

The wooden door was half ajar. Raised voices leaked from within. Pen opened it to hand Chio into the spacious vestibule, well-lit by lamps and wall sconces for receiving night emergencies.

The person arguing with the night porter was not some injured or, more likely tonight, wine-sick poor seaman. To Pen's astonishment, it was Learned Iserne. But a very different Iserne than the trim, brisk official he'd met this afternoon. Her black coat was hanging open over her dress, her sleek hair was escaping its pinned-up braids, and her face was drained and distraught. She near-vibrated with tension as she stood before the porter with all the air of a dog about to launch an attack.

She was accompanied by a young man apparently acting as her linkboy, for he held a walking-lantern in uneasy hands. He was dressed as a sober merchant, not a servant, though, in a gray jacket with pleated skirts to the mid-thigh, tight trousers, and a silver-studded leather belt for his knife. Lanky, typical Adriac coloration. His lips were pressed closed in distress, but he opened them to say, "Perhaps we should come back tomorrow, Learned Iserne."

She shot him a scorching look that silenced him again, and returned to the porter: "If Master Linatas is not here, there must be *someone* who has seen him. Night staff. Anyone."

Penric thought to pull his lion mask down, turning it to hang from the back of his neck. Chio kept her mask tied, pressing his arm and stepping half behind him. It seemed unlikely this was a sudden attack of shyness, but who knew. He gave her a reassuring nod and moved forward, interrupting the scene.

"Good evening. I'm Learned Penric, the Temple sensitive who was sent to Master Linatas to examine your mad castaway this afternoon, the one who ran off. I stopped in to see if he has been found or came back, or if you had any other word."

Iserne spun and stared at him in surprise. "Learned Penric! I was just thinking I might try to find you next."

"What's this all about?"

Iserne waved her expressive hands, but hardly seemed to know where to begin. A lawyer, at loss for words?

Her companion gave her a pitying glance, and cut in, "My name is Aulie Merin. I was riding share on the spring convoy to Cedonia, shepherding a mixed cargo for my employer. Learned Iserne's son Ree Richelon was aboard doing the same for his father. Our ship just returned home to Lodi this afternoon."

He inhaled, as if steeling himself. "I was charged with the heavy task of bearing the news to his family that Ree had been lost overboard in the night. Nearly a week ago, when we were beating up to our last stop in Trigonie. It seems heartless to encourage hope at this point, but..." He made a frustrated gesture at Iserne. "The shock. His mother."

"Did you search the water for him?" Pen asked.

Merin shook a regretful head. "Between the time he was last seen in the evening, and the time he was first missed in the morning, the convoy must have made fifty or sixty miles. There was no way."

"Was there a storm?"

"No, the night was clear, though the wind was brisk. No moon, so the deck was very dark."

Demanding a physical description of Merin's lost companion was going to be unhelpful, given Madboy's common looks. Pen had decanted the basics in front of his—maybe mother?—Iserne this afternoon without triggering recognition or alarm. Some hours before this news had arrived, to be sure, shattering her calm belief that her son was safely on his way home to her. Pen doubted the Bastard's Day was strongly celebrated in Iserne's household, as she had taken oath to a very different god, but likely any of her domestic thoughts had been pleasantly bent on a welcome-back dinner or some such thing. Pen had barely noticed Madboy's exterior, although he would recognize his demon-splintered soul at a hundred paces through a stone wall.

Pen turned back to the night porter. "Master Linatas has gone home for the day, you say? He left no messages for me, I take it?"

"That's right, Learned," he replied, relieved to face a less frantic interrogator.

"There must be others who worked directly with the shiplost patient you took in." The other men in the ward he'd so disrupted yesterday could also bear witness, but staff were more likely to handle distraught relatives smoothly. "Is Orderly Gnade still about?"

"I can send upstairs and see." The porter rose to call through one of the archways leading from the entry, to be answered by a young dedicat interrupted swallowing down a snack of bread. The lad scampered off up the stairs willingly enough.

Chio watched, quiet and attentive—aware?— as Pen extended his senses. Through the opposite archway, past closed doors, a few souls moved in a treatment room: a physician, hurting patient, assistant, and some anxious companion. No demons of any kind, so not Pen's affair.

Footsteps scuffing, plural; Pen looked up to find, thankfully, the page leading Gnade down to them.

"Oh," said Gnade, recognizing Penric. "You're the sorcerer fellow who came this afternoon and scared that poor mad boy into running off."

Pen ignored the second half of this, and hoped Iserne would, too. "I gather you've had no further word of him here?"

Gnade shook his head. "We did look, sir."

Pen turned to Iserne, whose slim hands were working in an anxious urge to interject, barely suppressed. "Did your son Ree have any particular identifying scars or tattoos, Learned?"

"Not—not when he left home." She looked to Merin. "Unless he acquired something on the voyage?"

"None I know of."

"What about clothing?" asked Chio, winning a curious glance from Merin, who had barely given notice to her till now.

Madboy had been dressed in, hm, a clean but worn shirt and trews with the look of the charity castoffs hospices reused for their patients. Pen asked, "He must have been wearing something when the fishermen brought him in, yes?"

"Not much," said Gnade, "but what the sea left you're welcome to examine, to be sure."

He was looking in puzzlement at Iserne, so Pen put in, "Learned Iserne here may be your patient's mother. She should see them." Although if Madboy had been wearing newer garments when he went overboard, that wasn't going to help either.

Gnade extracted a key from the porter, picked up a lamp, and motioned them through the left archway. The four visitors shuffled awkwardly after him, Chio again hanging back. Her silence masked a close listening, Pen thought.

Down the corridor, Gnade unlocked a door to what proved a small storage room, lined with shelving of plain sanded boards holding a miscellany of clothing and other possessions parted from their original owners. He set the lamp on the plank table in the middle and counted down the shelves. "I think we put them...ah, here."

He turned back with a scant pile of cloth and leather smelling of sea damp, and dumped them out. Iserne's companion stood back looking sick, but she dove upon them, hands rapidly sorting. She bit her lip, scowling in disappointment at an anonymous torn pair of trousers, a plain leather belt, the shreds of a shirt, and one stiff, rank sock. Her hand stopped short holding a salt-crusted embroidered handkerchief, and she bent to shove it into the pool of light and spread it out. "This was his. This was *Ree's*."

"Are you sure, ma'am?" asked the orderly. His even tone spoke of due care stemming from experience with upset relatives, rather than disbelief.

"I embroidered it myself. Then he's *alive!*" If Madboy—Ree, Pen corrected his thought—had been raised from the dead in front of them, her eyes could not have glittered more brightly with jubilant tears unshed. Her parted lips caught breath like a woman surfacing from drowning. "Saved from the sea, oh it *is* a miracle! One I didn't even know to pray for!"

If it was, it came with the kind of ambiguous catches for which Pen's god was noted. He cleared his throat. "This puts us very much further forward, but we still need to find him."

Merin looked up from the handkerchief and said plaintively, "I don't understand any of this! I thought the news I'd brought had turned her wits, and I shouldn't let her run off into the night here alone, but what's all this babble of demons and madness?"

"My wits are fine," snapped Iserne. "It's my *world* that's turned upside down."

The god of chaos and mischance, Pen reminded himself. He should know. "The man you lost overboard was found by a bedemoned dolphin, whose demon jumped to him. This is the one part of all this that was probably not an accident. Though you'll have to take my word for that. Ree would have experienced this invasion of his mind as a kind of madness. Maybe his exhaustion from trying to swim made him more susceptible, but in any case, the demon has ascended—possessed him. Long story, but while Temple demons are a benefit to their recipients, this wild one is effectively insane. When the fishermen picked Ree up, I'm sure it seemed he'd lost his reason altogether."

"Five gods." Merin signed himself, looking unnerved. "That's *bizarre*." He turned to Gnade. "Could he even talk?"

"Aye," said Gnade, "but there was no getting any sense out of him. Not even his name."

Merin huffed in horror. "Can he be cured?"

Pen glanced at Iserne, hanging on his words. He returned a firm "Yes," and concealed his gulp. *We'll make it so. Somehow.* "When he's found." He motioned Chio forward. She pushed up her feathered mask, baring her sobered face, and made a curtsey to Iserne, regarding the older woman intently. Less daunted by all these surging maternal emotions than Pen was? Or—odd perception— fascinated by them? Orphan, after all. "This is Blessed Chio, saint of the Bastard's chapterhouse on the Isle of Gulls, and my, er, colleague. When we find Ree, she will"—*eat the demon* maybe didn't sound reassuring.

No lie, muttered Des.

"Draw the demon from him," Pen continued smoothly, "by the grace of the white god. It may take him a while to recover from his physical ordeal and the shock to his mind, but with rest and quiet at home I'm sure he'll be all right in time." He nodded encouragement at Iserne.

Iserne stared at Chio in a surprise that turned to ferocious hope. "Really...?"

"Yes, Learned Iserne," said Chio with earnest politeness—rising to the occasion, or previously schooled by experience in dealing with distraught, confused...clients? Supplicants? Her usual guardians had likely handled the details. "I'll do all I can to help your son."

"Thank the gods."

Thank the white god, technically. But maybe not too soon.

"I'll help you search," Merin volunteered. He grimaced in guilt. "In exchange for the search I did not insist upon a week ago, at sea."

"I as well," said Iserne, her chin rising in determination.

Penric did not need the parade. Or even a link-boy. He temporized, "I think it would better serve if you were to return home, in case your son finds his way there."

Her head went back; her face lit. "Do you think he might?"

"By no means impossible. Ah..." The caution was painful but necessary. "There is a chance his ascended demon might feign to be him. If he does turn up, you should do nothing to alarm him, but secretly send for me at once."

She didn't like that one bit, but he thought she understood.

"Merin here can escort you home. Which is where, by the way?"

"It's not too far. We have a house on the Wealdmen's Canal, which empties out to the harbor between here and the state shipyard."

A decent address; not so elevated as the palaces of the merchant princes lining the main canal of the city, but an abode of hardworking men on the way up, or sometimes down.

"I really want to go with you," Merin told Penric, unhappily.

"Why don't we all escort Learned Iserne home," suggested Chio. "Then we'll know where it is for later."

This sensible compromise was adopted. With strongly worded instructions to the porter to send a message to the curia, regardless of the time, if anything new materialized here at the hospice, Pen led his enlarged party back out into the night.

ISERNE'S HOUSE lipped its canal. They had to circle past it to find a bridge, and then the narrower street that ran up to—Pen wasn't sure whether to think of it as the front or the back door. The dry door. They mounted steps behind Iserne to a second-story entry. The ground-or-canal floor presumably held the merchant husband's goods, with the living spaces above. She had a big iron key in her hand, but the door opened at her pull. "I don't suppose I thought to lock up when I ran out." She grimaced at this carelessness. She must have been going nearly as mad as Madboy in that moment, caught between the shock of grief and the greater shock of lunatic hope.

They entered the hallway to find it lit by dim wall sconces, and the brighter glow of a walking-lantern in the hand of a startled maidservant. Two young women clustered behind her looked equally disconcerted. "Mama," the elder or at least taller, who looked to be about Chio's age, said faintly. "We didn't know where you'd gone out to, or why…"

Best dresses, fetching white bows tied around their necks, and masks in their hands suggested this was not an incipient search party, but the other sort. Iserne had no trouble figuring it out either.

"I leave the house for an hour, and this is what you get up to?" Her voice was sharp, grating with real anger that seemed to take all three aback. These girls, clearly, had not yet been given the news about their brother, either version, before Iserne had rushed back out with her unhappy herald Merin.

"We were only just walking over to the party at the Stork Island chapterhouse," the younger protested. "Taking Bikka, and staying together! The divines of the white god will be there, giving blessings! It's safe!"

"Not that safe," said Iserne between gritted teeth. "And not *now*. I can't deal with any more chaos tonight..." She gripped her disarrayed hair and took a deep breath.

The elder looked up, discovering that there was a divine of the white god standing right in their hallway. She gaped only briefly at Pen and then Chio before her gaze went to Merin. "Ser Merin, you're back!" And more eagerly, "Is Ree with you? Is he still dealing with Father's cargo, or is he coming?"

Merin winced and gestured helplessly, tossing these unanswerable questions back to Iserne. He did produce a pained smile for the sisters.

"Lonniel, Lepia. Listen." Iserne's serious, strained voice caught both their attentions, their naughty excitement beginning to be quelled by unease. "Your brother is..." She faltered on the complexities, retreating to, "Very ill."

The elder—Lonniel?—gasped. "Where is he? Isn't someone bringing him home?" As all pleasure fled from her face, Pen could mark her wondering if *very ill* was a euphemism for *dead*.

Merin, with a glance at their hostess, cut in before Pen could. "He took a blow to the head from, from a crane as we were starting to unload. It seems to have scattered his wits. I think he might have been hallucinating, because he grew very frightened and didn't seem to recognize us. He ran off into the town, and now we're looking for him."

That's impressively glib, murmured Des.

Merchant. I suppose he had to learn to think on his feet. The tale did cover the essentials of the situation, erased of the uncanny and softened for the ears of the innocent.

True, but their mother should have been the one to make that choice, said Des.

He did take his cue from her lead-in.

Iserne's hands closed and opened in frustrated acceptance of this unasked-for aid. "I'll be waiting up for news, or in case he comes back here," she told the girls. "*You* two go to your beds and stay there." A scowl at the maid Bikka promised there would be another follow-up in her direction later.

With the perilousness of their brother's condition and their mother's upset impressed upon them, the sisters' mouths closed on mutiny, their shoulders slumping.

"I'm going out to search for him," Merin told both sisters, though his tense smile seemed aimed especially at Lonniel. "Even the Temple is lending us its aid, with Learned Penric here." He nodded in Pen's direction.

Lonniel touched her mouth, forming an *oh* at this explanation of their more baffling visitors. Looking over Pen and Chio, she said, "I'm sorry we have interrupted your holy eve with our affairs, Learned, and um—" Pen watched her trying to place Chio, and coming up with the notion they must be a couple out on the town, though uncertain whether the young lady's affections for the evening were paid or gratis. She settled on, "Miss. But please help Ser Merin all you may."

An attempt to straighten out this misconception of Pen's chain of command was not worth the delay, given the saint was merely smiling below her mask. She granted the other girls a friendly nod, returned with slight confusion.

Lepia put in, "But where could he have *gone,* hurt like that?"

"Not far, we hope," Merin told her. "With luck, we should have word by the time you wake in the morning."

Her face scrunched in her effort to imagine where her injured brother might try to den up. Pen would have liked to tax both sisters for ideas, given they'd probably know, hm, not more but different things of their sibling than even their mother did. Merin, since he was colleague, peer, and apparently family friend of Ree's, would possess yet another set.

But Iserne, reaching the limits of what Pen suspected was long patience, sternly drove the sisters up the stairs under the questionable supervision of their maid. Chio watched them ascend, her expression curiously covetous. A mother's chiding was still caring of a sort. Surely a saint was not subject to...envy?

As their steps echoed away, Iserne turned back to the entry hall, scrubbing her hands over her face as if to drive out numbness.

"Two hours ago," she told Penric, "I was going out of my mind trying to imagine how I was going to write my husband with the news of the death of our only son. This... I have no idea how I'm going to write this."

"Where is Ser Richelon?" Pen inquired.

"He travels every year up to the foot of the mountains to deal for timber. We supply some instrument and cabinet makers here in Lodi who have very particular needs. He usually goes later in the summer, but this year is the first that he let Ree take the spring convoy to Cedonia alone." She swallowed distress.

"I think you can safely put off that task till tomorrow," Pen said. "You should have more news by then. Better news, maybe." Risky promise.

"I suppose so." Iserne straightened and exhaled, her eye falling on a pile of objects dropped at the side of the hallway: several cases, a poniard in a tooled scabbard, and some loose clothing. "I could go through these and put them away while I wait. I'm not going to be able to sleep anyway."

"That was everything Ree left in our cabin," Merin told her. "It all fit on the one cart. Your husband's cargo is still aboard the ship, as there was no one to receive it. It will just have to wait there, since all the stevedores have gone off for the holiday by now, but I'll take on that task for you the day after tomorrow, if you wish."

Frowning, she waved away this offer. "I'll send Ripol's clerk."

Ripol? Merchant husband's first name, Pen decided.

She doesn't favor this fellow Merin, Des observed. *A case of beheading the messenger?*

Perhaps...

Iserne poked at the pile of cases with a tentative toe, possibly considering how much more painful her unpacking would be if their owner had been dead. Pen renewed his resolve to prevent that from becoming so.

"As far as I know," said Merin, "all of Ree's documents and letters of credit from the voyage are safe in there. I'm afraid his purse and money belt were on him when he went over the side. We didn't see either among his other things, later. I thought the belt had dragged him under—he'd had a very successful trip."

Neither item had been in the sad damp pile in the storage room, either, though sticky hands among those that had drawn Ree from the sea and delivered him to the hospice could have taken toll.

"Thank the gods he'd had the sense to drop it, rather than drown trying to keep it!" Iserne said fervently. "Just the sort of thing idiot brave boys attempt."

Merin offered a crooked smile. "I think my employer would have chastised me roundly for that."

"Hah." The maternal scorn in that syllable could have weighted a cudgel. "More fool he, since he'd have had neither money nor agent, after."

Since Iserne was as anxious as Penric for them to hurry the search, their farewells were brief.

"Blessed Chio." Iserne offered a clumsy curtsey; her supplication could not have been made more plain if she'd fallen to her knees. "The hope of my heart and house is in your god's hands tonight."

"It cannot be misplaced there, Learned." Gravely, Chio pulled her mask altogether off and returned her a full formal blessing, with the extra tap of the back of her thumb to her lips. It was the first trained gesture of their Order Pen had witnessed the girl make—Chio might have been as feral as a young elemental for all that Pen had seen heretofore.

Her face, as they descended the steps to the street again, had shed all its earlier merriment. She drew her mask back on, tightening the ties, as Merin raised his lantern and turned his head back and forth.

"Which way?"

Pen grunted. "I was hoping you might have some ideas. This wild demon, though ascendant, knew nothing of Lodi, so all the local navigation must be coming from Ree. Asking *Where would Ree go when in his right mind?* is probably not useful, but where would a man like him, or you, think to hide if he was in terror for his life?"

Merin blew out his breath. "Gods, what a question." The lantern sank to his side as he cogitated. "Lodi has a thousand alleys, all with corners and cubbies, and then there are all the interiors. Even if you stick to those that are unpeopled this time of night—shops and workshops, warehouses, government offices—probably not them—the central islands are circled by docks and wharves, and then there are all the outlying islands. This seems an impossible hunt."

"Not entirely. I only need to come within about a hundred paces of the demon to sense it, regardless of what walls or alleys or canals lie between." A sharp spike, somewhere in this buffeting phantasmagoria of the town's souls.

"How..." began Merin. "Never mind. But I don't quite understand what you do if we do find him."

Penric shrugged. "Hold Ree down as best I can without doing him injury, then let Blessed Chio call on our god. It should be a quick operation at that point." *I pray.*

"Will he be all right after that?"

"Exhausted, I'm sure." And grateful, Pen trusted. Un-Madboy had better be, after all this chase. "But then we can deliver him home and let Iserne take care of the rest."

"I see. I think." Merin frowned. "It sounds as if Ree was hard-battered by his ordeal in the sea. And the gods know what misadventures he's met since he escaped from the hospice. What happens if he dies before the saint can release him?"

"A greater mess than ever. I mean, over and above what the *dying* part would do to his family. Because the demon would jump to the closest other person it could reach, and we'd have the whole search to do over again, with even less information."

"But not to you? Or to Blessed Chio?" He made a newly nervy half-bow at the girl. "You'd need to be close for this, wouldn't you?"

"We're already occupied. Not sorcerers, not saints, not Wealdean shamans, though I wouldn't expect to encounter any of those in Lodi." Wealdean merchants, yes. "Anyone else in proximity would be at risk." Merin, for example. Really, the man was very much in the way.

"That...sounds really bad. Unless someone wanted a demon, I expect." His glance lingered, wondering, on Pen's shoulder braids.

"No one would want this demon," Pen assured him. "Most certainly not the Temple. Even though it would then be taking an imprint of Ree's memories with it overtop, it's still far too crazed to be tamed for any use."

Merin looked properly aghast, thinking this through. "Wait. It would *remember* Ree?"

"The next person it jumped to would. Think of it as like having the ghosts of all its prior possessors haunt your head, although that isn't theologically precise." He added, "And *talking* to you."

You needn't sound so put-upon, sniffed Des. *You enjoy our company.*

You still took some getting used to. The ten of you.

"Do these ghosts remember their deaths?"

"Vividly."

Merin's shoulders twitched in a cringe. "That sounds horrifying."

"One grows used to it."

His thick brows drew in. "Why don't demons go on forever?"

"Saints. And other accidents. There is attrition. Fortunately, or we'd all be up to our necks in them." *Instead of just my neck.* "That said, some can live a very long time, if they're carefully husbanded by my Order. My demon Desdemona is over two hundred years old."

Merin's expression hovered between impressed and appalled.

"Two directions, right or left," Chio prodded. "Pick one." She glanced back up the steps, her mouth pursing. "Needless delay seems much too cruel, right now."

Aye, agreed Des, and Pen was reminded that six of her riders had been mothers. He wondered if any of them had lost children.

In two centuries? We outlived all of them. In a sense.

Oh. I'd never quite thought that through.

Even now, we do not speak of that.

I see.

"Any guidance from your side yet?" Pen asked the saint.

"Not so far."

Of course not.

Pen tried to think what areas of these neighborhoods he'd already covered. He was losing track. Not that Madboy couldn't move about, so maybe it hardly mattered.

Merin pointed. "Left."

Pen shrugged and turned that way, leading them toward the middle of the muddled island neighborhood. Nothing in Lodi had a regular shape. Maybe he could find the center and spiral outward?

Scanning, walking, and talking at the same time risked stumbling over his own feet, but he asked Merin, "I take it you and Ree were thrown together as cabinmates. Had you known him and his family before?"

"Not as well as I got to know him shipboard. I used to work for one of his father's cousins, before I was hired away as an agent for this voyage, so I had some acquaintance." A longing sigh.

What's he pining for?

What, wasn't it obvious to you in Iserne's entryway?

I was following a great many things back there.

"So you were rivals with Ree, not partners?" Pen asked.

"Friendly rivals this time, yes. We might expect to be partners on some future venture. I'd hoped to work for Ser Richelon, who has a good reputation, but this other opportunity came up first."

Chio enquired slyly, "Does your current employer also have pretty daughters?"

Merin snorted, unoffended by the implication. "No, more's the pity. Among his other defects. Four strapping sons. A hired agent has no chance of moving up in that clan, no matter how hard-working."

Nor of marrying into it, obviously. Certain long-term relationships that came under the Bastard's thumb could be economically similar, one type of close partnership cloaked by another, but Pen hadn't noticed Merin's eye being caught by anyone not female, so far. To his personal relief. Pen favored round girls, given his choice—though not, alas, the otherwise personable Chio. Her *randomly channels a demon-eating god* aspect was too daunting.

Thank you, murmured Des. *One of your infatuations in that direction would have been supremely awkward.* Pen's lips twitched.

Chio observed to Merin, "I thought you fancied Sera Lonniel, just now."

In the glow of the walking-lantern, Merin's cheeks darkened in a sheepish blush. He ducked his head. "Who wouldn't? Just on marriageable age, respectable house—her parents guard her very closely, though, so it makes her hard for a poor man to court. Ree was—is—will be again, I hope, good company, but on that point he's just as stiff as his learned mother."

Ah. Iserne's distaste illuminated? Rich daughter, poor suitor, a common tale.

Merin's jaw set. "A sufficient fortune of my own could overcome all those barriers, if I can ever gain it."

"Your own family isn't in trade?" said Pen.

"No. I'm from a farming village in the Adriac hinterland. The usual tale, too many siblings, and the younger turned out like stray cats to seek their own fates."

As the seventh and lastborn in his own family, Pen could sympathize. Although his fate had sought him, as nearly as he could tell. Or perhaps his god's left hand.

Pish, said Des. *You would never have been happy in that narrow mountain valley, even as its shabby lord.*

Less even than as its youngest scion, Pen reflected. *I was entirely content to leave those dreary duties to my eldest brother.* Who appeared to be content to have them, so a win all around.

"At least," Chio remarked to Merin, "they didn't drown you like a sack of kittens."

Foundling, right. Unwanted bastards left on the white god's doorstep were the *lucky* ones. The canals of Lodi swallowed many secrets, to be flushed out on the tides.

A flash of bitterness from Merin: "No, they send us to Lodi and let the city destroy us for them."

Penric had read the man as an unhappy soul from the beginning, but this appeared to go deeper than the disaster to his cabinmate that had been dumped on his hands. Right now, though, Pen had other souls to attend to. Too many, everywhere, and all the wrong ones. Still. The trio—four, counting Des—fell silent for a time, pacing along the maze. Pen's feet were starting to hurt.

The alleys grew quieter as people with duties tomorrow, religious or otherwise, drew in for the night. Though Lodi's prostitutes did not seem to be taking their holiday off; they passed a few such squeezed into dark niches actively pursuing their trade. Pen shifted Chio to his other side, but she seemed neither shocked nor afraid.

"Of course not," she murmured at his anxious query. "Those boys are too busy jumping their ladies to jump us. It's the unattached bravos you have to watch out for."

Shrewd girl, Des approved.

Chio glanced over her shoulder at the lewd noises fading in the shadows, and remarked, "Those poor street whores are not so valued by the city. They're harder to squeeze taxes out of than their sisterhoods in the brothels and bordellos. It's said that the levies paid by the ladies of Lodi fund the building of a state galley every year. *I* think those ships should be named for famous courtesans, but they keep naming them after boring old men instead."

Pen was surprised into a bark of laughter, imagining an imposing warship named *Mira of Lodi* gliding over the waves.

It would overawe all rivals, Des assured him smugly.

He sobered, considering Chio's insights. The denizens of the Bastard's orphanages must have a rough view of the backside of the colorful tapestry that was Lodi. Chio might play a sheltered maiden most convincingly, when it suited her, but she was not one. Even without that hidden portal on infinite space she had tucked secretly about her.

They came to a halt at an alley mouth that gave onto another market, illuminated by what table lanterns hadn't run out of oil and the dancing flames of a cresset, its iron basket held up on a post beside the canal landing. Sinuous yellow-orange lines reflecting in the dark water danced back.

The party hosted here had reached the latest stage of devolution: families gone, young and unattached older men getting drunk, drunker, or drunkest, throwing up or pissing into the canal, loud verbal fights with each other edging toward brawls. Those women yet present, some of them as drunk as their partners, were either plying their trade or else just being very bawdy.

Pen would have been content to edge around this mob, but Chio raised her chin and sniffed the lack of breeze. "Ooh. That fellow still has meat sticks for sale. Let's get some. We can eat them as we walk on, and not need to stop."

One of the last remaining vendors apart from the wine booth supervised an iron basin of coals on a tripod, topped with a grille where he turned sizzling skewers. Their smoke might be the only appetizing smell left curling through the damp midnight air. Pen's suddenly watering mouth reminded him that they hadn't eaten for hours, and they would both need their strength if—when—they caught up with Madboy. *Feed the saint* was certainly part of his Temple duties tonight, eh?

He waved an amiable assent to Chio and threaded his way toward the enticing tripod, where he had to wait for the preceding customers.

'Ware cutpurse, murmured Des.

This square being demon-free, Pen had gratefully eased Des's extended senses, but he flared them a little now. The back of his neck crawled in expectation of a very sharp knife slicing the cord of his purse, in preparation for some drunken-seeming collision later where he would be relieved of it. But to his astonishment, the hand rose to his shoulder braids. A butterfly landing upon him would have had no more weight.

Pen was so boggled, he almost gave the man another few seconds just to see if he would succeed in his delicate unpinning operation. He was fairly certain the answer was *yes*.

Sadly, no. Pen reached up, seized the pickpocket's wrist, and turned in one smooth motion, yanking the man forward. A reach, a sorcerer-physician's precise twist to the axillary nerve—not hard enough to snap it, but enough to leave the whole arm limp and stinging.

"Was this a dare or a death-wish?" Pen breathed in the man's ear.

"Dare!" he squeaked. "Pardon, pardon, learned sir! Just a prank! Forgiveness on our god's day!"

No question that this was no prank, but the man's trade—he'd been far too adept for an amateur thief. From the corner of his eye, Pen spotted a couple of his probably-colleagues, who had been watching the show and grinning, retreat hastily into the shadows at this abrupt reversal of fortune. Pen could imagine the conversation that had led up to this—*I wager I can lift the braids right off that skinny sorcerer's shoulder!* If Pen had been any other sort of Temple divine, he likely could have.

Servile, grinning, and terrified, an unsavory combination. Pen took a deep breath to calm himself, and continued his sermon at a whisper's range. "Your hand will be useless for a day. If I chose to take you to a city constable, it would be removed altogether. Consider this foretaste a god-given chance to pray and reflect on your poor choice of callings. Some craft where your fifth mistake won't result in your hand being amputated would be good. You have skill. Use it for better ends."

Pen released his assailant-turned-victim, who backed away bobbing bows and babbling apologies until he could turn and scamper.

Pen sighed. *Do you think my homily will take, Des?*

Hard to say. Impressive try, though. Demonic amusement. *On both your parts.*

Pen wondered if *Don't drink and rob!* would have been more pointed advice. It wasn't as if he didn't have two spare sets of braids in his clothes chest.

He fished his purse from under his coat and shirt, thankful to find it still there, and settled up for three skewers of meat. Aromatic with garlic, otherwise not very identifiable; *browned* sufficed tonight. A stop at the wine booth for something red and redolent to wash it down would delay them, but it was tempting. Toasted sticks in hand, he looked around for Chio and Merin.

They were gone.

HE WAS *puzzled.* Not *alarmed,* Pen told himself and his leaping pulse as he swept the square with his gaze. Chio's showy striped dress should stand out even in flickering shadows. *No luck.* He flashed Des's demonic sense to its fullest range. By now, he could recognize those souls at a distance much as one would recognize the form of a friend seen down the street. Nothing.

He wheeled, checking the square again. The cut-purse and his cronies were gone, naturally enough. He didn't see how they could have taken Chio and Merin with them by force without his or Des's notice in the few moments he'd spent collecting the meat. Nor why, actually.

No, agreed Des. But when a *demon* sounded worried...

The canal here had no footpath, lapping right up to the buildings on either side. The sole access was by oarboat at the market landing. Water traffic had thinned out, only a few hardy boatmen still circulating to ferry inebriated customers home.

This market had three dry entries, the alley they'd come in by, and the other two leading who-knew-where—just because they started off in one direction didn't mean they'd continue that way.

Pen picked the wider, cobbled one and trotted down it, frugally munching his meat skewer. The snack didn't settle well in his newly nervous stomach, despite his peckishness. After a hundred paces, the street narrowed and ended in a close-built ring of houses. A Lodi rat could have escaped between them, but not a girl in a party dress and whoever she'd left with. Merin must be accompanying her, Pen reasoned with himself, his pulse, and his digestion. Chio could not be completely unprotected.

I've lost the saint! Envisioning himself explaining this to Learned Riesta, Pen fought panic. She was only temporarily mislaid, surely.

Back to the market. Taxing a few bleary men and the less bleary vendors for witness bore no fruit; the first had been too drunk and the second too busy keeping them so. Pen scowled at the time he'd lost and headed into the final street. In a minute, the first crossing presented him with the usual three-way dilemma.

Pen halted, thinking of his late father's description of a dog trying to chase two rabbits. Doomed to catch neither, in the paternal parable. Increasingly frantic circling was not the answer. He'd been doing that all night.

If the pair hadn't been kidnapped, one must have persuaded the other away. But which? He wouldn't put some impulsive start past Chio, certainly. Earlier in the evening, he might have imagined her growing bored with her stodgy Temple protector and haring off to find a better party, but not since their sobering encounter with the distraught Iserne. So she must have had a reason. A god-inspired reason? Attempting to picture what, or how, made him want to gibber.

The notion of Merin luring her away from Penric also left him at a loss. Not slyly divesting a romantic rival of his prize; he'd shown no hint of being interested in Chio that way, although it would take a brave man to approach a saint.

Or the penniless orphan *part accounts for his lack of ardor*, Des put in.

Would Iserne concur with her? But no, Merin had been as intent on their pursuit as the rest of them. Pen had not misread that.

"Des, what do you make of Merin?"

The impression of a doubtful *Hmm. I see souls. I don't hear their thoughts as you and I hear each other's, you know that. Handy as that god-like gift would be. He's upset, but then he would be. More determination than malice, and more fear than either. Much more fear. For Ree, and unease at his dangerous situation, I'd thought.*

Thus Merin, regardless of the details of his motivation, would still be set on finding Ree. So... maybe Pen wasn't chasing two rabbits. Maybe there was only one, or in any case two going in the same direction. *Where haven't I searched yet?*

He reviewed his routes around a mental map of Lodi. The city was ten times the size of Martensbridge, itself ten times the size of Pen's mountain home of Greenwell Town, but he'd chewed through most of it by now. He hadn't covered any of the outlying islands except the Isle of Gulls, though how a penniless madman could contrive to get across the lagoon defeated even Pen's imagination.

I really don't think he'd have tried to swim, said Des. *Dolphin-haunted or not.*

Agreed.

Oh. There was one place Pen hadn't examined; the harbor shore near the hospice, apart from the bits along the route between the hospice and Iserne's house. Because it had already been searched in that first hour by Linatas and Tebi—looking for a madman and a fuss. Could the bedemoned Ree instead have hidden himself from their view in the marine clutter? *Easily.* Pen would have spotted him regardless, but ordinary eyes might not.

Pen swore aloud in Wealdean at this potential miss.

Though if Merin had been seized by some late inspiration of a new place to look for his lost cabinmate, why hadn't he brought the thought to Penric? Pen was liking this less and less. He walked on into the darkness that wasn't dark to him, somewhat vengefully consuming Merin's meat stick. And, in the twenty minutes it took him to backtrack through the stone and water maze to the harbor, Chio's as well, though mainly to free his hand. Her penalty for running off without telling him.

Trying to be systematic, always a challenge in Lodi, Pen angled through to the shoreline on the far side of the hospice and worked his way back up toward the state shipyard. There were a surprising number of souls about in the after-midnight darkness, and not just celebrants staggering home. Sailors slept out on their moored ships. Others denned up in various cubbies and shacks. Pen passed a pair of night watchmen, more looking for fires than criminals though prepared to sound an alarm for either.

One lifted his lantern and frowned at Pen, glimmering gold-white in the pool of light. Seeing a divine's coat and braids, and of the fifth god's Order on His night, he bobbed his head in nervous respect. "Learned sir. You're out late."

"Unfortunately yes. I'm looking for a, uh, sick man who might have come through here. Also for a young couple..." Pen described his missing trio, leaving out the lengthy explanation. Which made it all rather mysterious; the watchmen regarded him with misgiving. But they had not seen any of the people Pen was looking for since they'd come on duty at nightfall. Pen left them with a parting blessing anyway, which they accepted with scarcely less worry.

He searched as far as the mouth of the Wealdmen's Canal without luck, then had to circle up it for the bridge. This brought him back down Iserne's street and past her steps. He did not stop in; Des's Sight told him that Ree had not returned here. Lamplight leaked through third-story shutters from the wakeful woman waiting.

Needless delay would be cruelty... He would run, if he'd known what way.

Back to the harborside. The next stretch was mainly devoted to the use of Lodi fishermen like the ones who'd first trawled up Madboy. Tackle, festoons of nets drying, crates, fish-traps, and boats small enough to be pulled ashore for the night made a maddening obstacle course through damp sand. A few craft were upside down, waiting repairs or maintenance on their hulls. If Pen hadn't been looking with Des's Sight, he would never have spotted the man tucked beneath one. Not Madboy, not Merin. Fisherman? Vagabond? No... *What's wrong with him?*

Quite a lot, said Des uneasily, *but not our affair, surely...?*

Pen knelt and peered into what would be black shadow to anyone else. The fellow breathing in stertorous gasps was neither sleeping nor drunk. He'd taken a plank to the head. Crawled under there himself, or been rolled in? Robbed?

Comprehensively, murmured Des.

He was wearing nothing but his drawers. He might be in his twenties, sailor or merchant or anything, but he didn't look starveling so probably not a street beggar. Pen didn't wonder *Who would rob a beggar?* since the answer was *Anyone with fewer possessions and more desperation.* Wanting clothes, in this case. And a purse? Pen set his teeth, got a grip on clammy ankles, and dragged the fellow out from under the downturned oarboat.

His dark hair was clotted with blood, mostly dry. So, the injury suffered about two hours ago? The profusely bleeding scalp wound had been superficial, the concussion less so. His skull was not fractured, though, and the bleeding seemed to be confined to the outside, fortunately.

Pen could afford a strong dose of general uphill magic against the shock, brain bruising, and blood loss at no more cost than the life of one of the harbor rats, which were ready to hand, skulking in the shadows. It was a wonder none had taken a nibble of the fellow so far. Pen drew breath and called up this most-practiced basic healing skill, trying hard not to think of all the grievous times it had failed him. He wasn't *doing* this anymore, so why was he doing *this...*?

Des made her silence a dry-enough comment.

Pen quelled the shiver of raw mortal memories as order passed out through his hands into the hurting body, trading for slightly greater disorder flowing up into him.

His...patient, foundling, emitted a groan. Pen searched around for a splinter of wood, stuck it upright in the sand, and set it alight with a touch. This makeshift candle wouldn't last long, but it didn't need to. When the fellow pried open his sticky eyelids, he would be able to see more than a threatening silhouette looming over him.

He stretched his jaw, raised a hand to his head; a gleam of dark eyes at last shone up. They widened at Pen. "Am I dead?" the man croaked.

He might have been by morning, if the rats had found him. "Happily not."

"...thought you might be the white god come to collect me. Wondered what I'd done wrong."

"No, just His errand boy."

"Good. M' mother wouldn't have liked that..." Fingers poked gingerly through matted, crusty hair.

"You took a bad knock, though," said Pen. "Any idea who gave it to you?" He was getting an unsettling notion about that.

The fellow was momentarily distracted as his wandering hands discovered his near-naked state. He swore. "My good doublet!" Bony feet felt each other. "My good boots! You 'spect to lose your purse, but who steals a man's *breeches?*" A moment later: "Gods, I feel sick…" He spasmed; Pen helped him roll over to vomit. There had been a wine party earlier, evidently. "Ohh, Mother of Summer help me…"

"I'll bring you to the Gift of the Sea hospice shortly," Pen promised. "As soon as you think you can walk."

A whuff, possibly grateful.

"Did you see who robbed you?" Pen asked again.

"Only f' a moment. 'S coming home up the harbor street about an hour before midnight—what time s'it now?"

"About an hour after, I make it." Not the worst swoon, though such were never good.

"Barefoot young man by himself. Mumbling. Thought he was too drunk to be a danger, didn't pay much mind as he went by. Then I saw stars. The next thing, you." He pushed himself up on one elbow and looked around, wincing and blinking, then sank back with another groan. "Not far from here."

"What did he look like?"

"About my height and size, I guess. A bit younger? Pretty ragged, so it was hard to tell. Not much light."

"Hair?"

"Dark, tangled."

Pen repeated the somewhat useless physical description of Ree Richelon.

The stripped fellow shook his head, then clutched it. "Ow. I…maybe?"

Not obviously *Not*, then. Pen passed his hand over the victim. No signs of demonic disruption—he didn't think Madboy understood the theological hazards of magical violence, but perhaps the plank or chunk of spar or whatever had seemed weapon enough.

But if it *had* been Madboy, that meant he'd still been here in the area not two hours ago. Though also that he had amended his purseless and unclothed state, and gained more ability to move about or escape.

Not over the causeway till it opens again at dawn, though, Des put in. *He's trapped in Lodi tonight unless he goes by boat.*

The stolen money would aid that, although not many boats were still moving at this hour, Bastard's

Eve or not. Not that he couldn't just seize a small boat, if he was strong enough to drag it to the water by himself. Or simply untie it from a dock, though their owners usually took in their oars for the night to thwart such thefts.

"How much was in your purse?" Pen asked.

It took bashed-man a dizzied moment to follow the question. "Less'n I'd started out with tonight. Never thought I'd be glad to *lose* at play."

"What color was your doublet?"

The man squinted at him in further confusion. "What? ...Wine-red, I sup'ose. Good cloth. Only second time I'd worn it." He sighed regret.

In a few minutes, Pen was able to urge the man to his feet, one arm hoisted over Pen's shoulder, though the movement made him shudder with renewed nausea. They staggered along bumping hips up to the paved harbor street, where Pen prepared to retrace his steps, fretting. He'd traded too much time for these ambiguous clues. Though he supposed he qualified as the Bastard's luck tonight to the robbery victim. He'd have to suggest a donation to his Order.

They'd not limped very far when they encountered another pair of night watchmen. Relieved, Pen traded off his foundling to them with instructions to take him to the Gift of the Sea.

"Tell them Learned Penric sent him, and that he may have something to do with a problem I'm working on for them," he instructed the watchmen. "They'll understand. My Order will cover his fees, if it's required."

This last barely reconciled them to their unexpected and out-of-their-way chore; getting the hint, Pen tipped a couple of coins into their palms to assure the concussed fellow's safe arrival. His slurred voice drifted back still mourning his doublet as Pen turned and strode toward the state shipyard.

Despite the cooling night air, he was sweating from his magical exertion. *Magical friction,* Learned Ruchia had dubbed it in her book on fundamentals of sorcery. Which he'd planned to spend the past afternoon continuing to translate into Adriac. He gritted his teeth. "Des, a rat. Or something."

A brief survey. Over there. In the black shadow of a drain, a blacker movement. At least it was one of the big, ugly, corpse-chewing harbor rats, and thus not distressingly cute. The creature squeaked and died as Pen divested the healing's dregs of disorder into it. Passing on, Pen tapped his lips with the back of his thumb in dutiful thanks to his god for the sacrifice of one of His creatures.

Pen's stride lengthened. Blessed Chio had been out of his sight for far too long. And while he wouldn't have minded losing Merin, could the fool have abandoned her somewhere? *Not good, not good.*

He came to his next check along the harbor street. Another canal bisected it, a stubby channel leading only to a small basin ringed by goods sheds and warehouses. The buildings shouldered tightly together, each with its own water gate closed and locked for the night. The water glimmered against their black bulks. He was just trying to see a way past when Des said tightly, *Found 'em.*

Bastard be thanked! Finally! He whipped his attention around and followed her Sight.

Three souls: Merin, Chio, and the fractured, pained, demon-ridden being he'd glimpsed so vividly at the hospice. This—no, yesterday afternoon, now. All were together. Distress, anger, and fear were as thick as a fog around them. *Where...?* They appeared to be within a warehouse on the opposite side of the pool. And something bad was going on. The cornered Madboy attacking the saint? Even Pen could not run across the water to get to it directly. He'd have to go around.

He could still run. Expecting the road to ring it for access on the dry side, he snarled in frustration to find it led on into the city instead. He spotted a narrow passage between two houses and turned sideways, scuttling through it to the street opposite. This one led back to the harbor and the goods sheds on the farther arc of the basin.

The warehouse's double door was locked, barred from the inside. The only other visible access was a door on the second floor leading onto air, a crane affixed above it for lifting goods up and down. Des could undo locks. Bars were heavier and trickier. Winded, Pen bent to examine the mechanism.

Chio's screech—Pen wasn't sure if it was in fear or rage—moved him instantly to a more brutal approach, magic and a mighty kick combined. Lock, bar, and door burst inward, followed by Pen. He looked wildly around.

Bundles, bales, and lumber blocked his view. An orange glow rose beyond them. Pen caromed through the narrow aisles to an open space for marshaling cargo by the water door. Merin's walking-lantern, sitting on a nearby crate, illuminated a confusing scene.

Merin and Madboy were locked together in a furious scuffle. Not a wonder in itself; with the saint present, the demon was fighting for its life. The disheveled Chio orbited the pair just out of range. Her mask was hanging, her hair was half-down, and a fresh red bruise marred her cheek.

Merin had his belt-knife in hand, gripping a pewter pitcher in the other by way of a makeshift shield. Madboy was armed with a longer poniard, no doubt lifted from the same source as the red doublet, breeches, and boots he now wore.

"You murderer. You cowardly thief," snarled Madboy. As accusations went, this seemed to Pen oddly turned-around. Steel clanged off pewter.

"Chio!" Merin bellowed desperately. "Do it, do it, you idiot bitch! Hurry!"

She yelled back, "I don't call the god like a dog! He comes when He chooses! I've *explained* that!"

To, or through, tranquil, emptied souls, Pen had thought. Which Chio's wasn't, in this frenzied moment.

Exhaustion and despair can work as well as tranquility, Des put in.

Aye, not those either.

As the wrestling pair turned, Merin's eye fell on Pen. "Oh, gods, *he's* here!"

Not the joy at rescue Pen would have expected; more a voice of loathing. *Mad demon first, mysteries later.*

At least nothing was on fire, yet. This demon seemed slow to deploy even the most basic magics, but maybe dolphins didn't think in terms of arson.

The two fighters sprang apart, gasping for air. Circled for another opening as if revolving on a rope.

As the demon fought his friend Merin, Ree ought to be impeding it as best he could, beyond just the bodily fatigue of his sea ordeal sapping demonic speed and strength. Jerks and feints and stumbles, other hindrances. Instead, the two seemed of one mind, equally intent upon their attacker. *When both surrender to one desire...*

This demon likewise should have been attending to its greater threat from the Temple sorcerer, not following its mount's impassioned focus on Merin. It was leaving itself wide open, and Pen did not delay.

Two anatomically expert nerve twists, one to the right hand and the other to the left leg. The poniard dropped from paralyzed fingers, and Madboy's leg folded under him, dumping him to the floor. He cried out in pain.

Merin lunged for him. Pen lunged faster, wrapping his arms around the man and trapping his knife hand. "That's enough, Merin! It's over. He's down."

Merin wrenched, then went still. After a cautious moment, Pen released him.

"Oh," said Chio in a peeved tone. "*Now* He shows up." She shoved back her hair and braced her spine, as if lifting a burden.

Stepping forward, she placed her hand on Madboy's brow. Pen could track the arrival of the god by the departure of Des, who, with no other escape, curled into a tight, terrified ball inside him. He granted her the retreat, but he wished she wouldn't take most of her perceptions and all of her powers along, leaving Pen disarmed of his magics.

Chio took a deep breath, opened her mouth, and gulped. Pen had just enough Sight left to feel the demon being drawn out of Ree and into her, and on to the god, in a hideous, frantic, spiky stream. Madboy's anguished howl ran down abruptly as his possessor was torn from him, turning into Ree's very human groan.

"Ugh," choked Chio. "That's a bad one. Just awful." She swallowed and swallowed again, as if trying not to throw up.

With all the hours and sweat and shoe leather spent getting Blessed Chio into position for this confrontation, the actual...miracle, Pen conceded, was the work of a moment. Miracle, murder...putting-to-dissolution, he supposed. The saint was an executioner who wasn't getting this Bastard's Day off.

A flash in Pen's mind, but not his eyes, a sense of endless vertigo an instant in duration but infinite in depth, and the god departed with His prize, a strange perfume lingering in His wake that might have been a whispered, *Well done, my lovely Child.*

Pen wasn't sure. It hadn't been to his address. He couldn't have withstood any more direct exposure than that. But Chio's plain face shone with a fleeting inner light of heartbreaking beauty. *Numinous,* Pen supposed, was the precise theological term. The word seemed wholly inadequate.

Single-minded again, Ree gaped up in awe at Blessed Chio, swaying on her feet. "*Oh...!*" Breathed like a prayer. As it should be.

Merin swung his head back and forth as if expecting Madboy to rise and attack again. Penric knelt to the de-demoned youth, hoping he hadn't hurt him too severely. He knew he hadn't snapped the throbbing nerves, so they should settle down in a while, an hour or a day, he wasn't sure. His back half-turned, his demon not recovered from her brush with the holy, he only barely caught Merin's motion as he raised his knife and dove forward. At *Penric.*

"What—!"

"No!" shrieked Chio, and threw her shoulder forward into Merin as though trying to batter down a door. It unbalanced him enough that his first stab missed, grazing Pen's sleeve instead of plunging into his back. Pen fell to his hands, scrambling.

Eyes white-rimmed, teeth bared, Merin turned to this unexpected hazard from his flank. His knife flashed in the lantern light, gripped for a lethal thrust. Weaponless, Chio whipped her remaining hair stick out of her braid and brandished it. Merin looked at it and scoffed.

Pen regained his feet. *Des, blast it—!* "What are you doing, you lunatic?" he yelled at Merin. Was the man overcome by some blinding battle frenzy, unable to tell friend from foe? He seemed to have gone wilder than Madboy. "This fight is over!" He started forward to again restrain him.

"Not nearly," Merin gasped, and lunged once more at Penric. Pen had only his own speed to evade the blade, and maybe he'd been sitting in libraries too much lately—

Whereupon both combatants discovered that a thin, six-inch-long steel rod, with the full weight of an angry young woman behind it, had quite enough power to go completely through a man's upper arm and tack it to his torso. Unsharpened point or not. Merin yowled and dropped his knife, clawing at the glittering glass knob with his other hand. Chio yelped and retreated as Merin staggered and swung his free arm viciously at her.

At *last*, Des's powers flooded back into Penric. Pen reached out with her magics and twisted *both* of Merin's sciatic nerves, just to be sure. As excruciating agony seized his legs, he flopped to the floor, screaming.

You're late, Pen panted to his demon.

Sorry...

"What," Penric began, but doubted he could be heard over Merin's cries echoing off the wooden rafters. He grimaced, bent forward, and touched the man's throat, then had to reach again as he thrashed away. Paralyzing the vocal cords without blocking breath was a delicate task that he wouldn't have dared from any greater distance. The screaming didn't exactly stop, but it grew unvoiced, a wheezing series of gasps.

"That's better," said Chio in a shaken voice.

"Yes," rasped Pen as his ears stopped ringing. He stood catching his breath and his scattered wits.

"I'd wondered why I didn't like him." She touched the red mark on her face. Wait, was that the work of Madboy or Merin? *Until the god is upon me, and then I see everything*, she'd said, and Pen believed her. What inner worlds had she just seen here?

Pen turned to her, his eye taking in Ree as well, who was clumsily sitting up trying to work his numb hand. "But Bastard's teeth, *what* was going on here? No, start with—why did you two run off from me at the marketplace?" He pointed one cautious toe at Merin, squirming and mouthing like a landed fish.

"He suddenly said he'd guessed where Ser Richelon would be hiding," Chio said, vexation coloring her voice. "Then he grabbed me"—she rubbed her forearm; Pen scowled to see young bruises forming up in the pattern of fingerprints—"and bundled me into an oarboat that had just pulled up to let off another passenger. He told the boatman to take us to the harbor. I expected you to follow on with your Sight, so I didn't cry out or protest—I didn't think I needed to. I mean, I wanted to get to the demon, and he was taking me to the demon." She looked around, and asked Ree, "What exactly is this place, Ser Richelon, and why were you here? Because Ser Merin was right about that part."

Still shaky with pain, Ree gestured distractedly. "This warehouse is shared by my father and my uncle. His cousin, but I call him my uncle. When Merin was employed by him, we both worked here, sometimes. Then he left, and we didn't meet again till we were thrown together on the spring convoy. You two know about that?" He twisted toward Pen. "You're that scary sorcerer from the hospice—of course you must, if you came for me. You and the god. And the...saint?"

From the stunned-ox air Ree bore as his gaze returned to Chio, Pen grasped that he'd had an intimate view of his miracle. And of that holy execution. How much had he felt of his ascendant demon's destruction? And had it been release, horror, awe, or all three inextricably mixed?

Des shuddered.

"This felt like a safe place to hide, and I knew how to get in," Ree went on.

Looks like Merin remembered how, too, said Des. *With less destruction to doorways.* Her regret for the front entry was entirely feigned, Pen judged.

"I didn't have much control, but I dreaded the demon getting any nearer to my mother and sisters. Do you know about them? Oh…" Ree looked down at his red sleeve in fresh worry, then up at Penric. He quavered, "Learned sir, I think… I think I might have killed a man earlier tonight. I know I robbed him."

So, Ree remembered Madboy's acts. This was going to be interesting. "Put your heart at ease," Pen advised him. "The man survived, and will recover. You may even get a chance to return his things." As Ree continued to look distraught, he added, "The Temple, or at least my Order, will know it wasn't you, and will speak on your behalf if it comes to that."

Chio wrinkled her nose. "How do you even *know* that the man…never mind."

Ree blew out his breath in a mixture of turmoil and relief. "It was all so confusing till just now. Like the worst fever dream ever." His gaze caught again in wonder on Chio.

"I daresay," said Pen. "Ah—why was Merin trying to kill you?"

"Trying to kill me *again*, rather." Ree's black brows drew down in anger. Wrenching aside from his worship, he glared in Merin's direction. "He'd thrown me off our ship to drown."

"Why?" asked Chio. She didn't sound shocked.

"I'd spotted him stealing his master's funds." His voice heated. "More fool I, I'd thought I could talk him into putting the money back, and then I wouldn't tell anyone, and all would be right again. That's why I took him out on the deck alone in the night. First he tried to bribe me, as if I would—! Then he saw a more certain way to shut me up."

"In the panic of a fight?" asked Pen.

"We did fight, but he knocked me woozy. He was cool enough to take my purse before he tipped me over the side rail, though." His lips tightened in remembered outrage.

"How frugal." *Premeditation enough, I daresay.* "A money belt was mentioned—did he take that too?"

"I kept that locked in a chest in my cabin. I don't know if he found it later." Ree looked suddenly even more worried. "Its key was in my purse. He knew that."

"If he filched it, it should be discovered in his things when this incident is investigated," Pen suggested. "I don't know about your father, but if it's lost I can promise you your mother won't care."

"You've met my mother?" Ree's eyes sprang wide, and he gasped in new alarm. "Oh gods, they'll have told my family I drowned!" He lurched, trying to rise. "I have to get home!"

Chio knelt to him and made soothing murmurs, patting his shoulder as if he were a restive horse till he settled back, still panting anxiously.

The disjointed tale laid bare Merin's formerly baffling motives, though. Cold greed, and hot fear of being found out. Should fear be added to the list of great sins?

It can do as much harm, I'll grant, said Des.

A STIFF voice called from the wrecked doorway, "Hey! What's going on in there?" Wary footsteps resolved into two men in the tabards of the state shipyard—its lords administrative kept a full roster of watchmen in the area, even or perhaps especially on holiday nights, so Pen was less taken aback than they were. One held up a lantern; the other had his short sword out and ready. "We heard screaming."

Well, here's trouble, said Des.

Not necessarily. It all depends on how I play it.

I yield this hand to you, Temple-man. By all means go be Learned Sir at them.

Chio shrank back beside Ree. Pen stepped forward, and said heartily, "Five gods be thanked you're here!" The sword sank only slightly. Lantern-man put his other hand on the truncheon hung at his hip.

"We interrupted an attempted murder," Pen went on, which didn't seem to reassure them. Leaving aside the question of who had been trying to murder whom when Pen first had come in. Merin had certainly been bent on getting rid of witnesses, but had been blocked by the problem of the demon until the saint had done her deed—Pen had to give him credit for paying attention to his demon-lectures.

The whole growing, teetering pile of lies and crime tonight must have been cobbled together impulsively as Merin tried to work around the unexpected god-gift of Ree's survival and demonic possession. Add *rashness* to his list of defects. If he'd managed to dispatch Ree, would he have gone on to Chio? *Where would he hide the bodies?* was hardly a problem in canal-laced Lodi. The picture made Pen sick. *My Lord Bastard, you trim your timing far too fine.*

For this audience, Pen decided to stick with more recent and clear events. "This man"—he pointed down at Merin—"just made an ill-advised attempt to stab me." True enough. "Ah, permit me to introduce myself. I'm Learned Penric kin Jurald, court sorcerer to Archdivine Ogial."

Ree's eyes widened. So did the watchmen's, though they maintained a properly suspicious stance. In Lodi, Ogial's was a name to conjure with even if one wasn't a sorcerer.

"And this is my colleague and saint of my Order, the Blessed Chio," Pen went on, moving possessively to the girl's side as she rose.

He'd been making headway up to that point, but received a look of narrow disbelief as they took in the details of the alleged saint: a rumpled young female who might have been a bedraggled festival-goer, prostitute, victim of attempted assault sexual or otherwise, or all of them at once. Chio raised her decided chin and cast them a credible look of disdain in turn. But she shifted closer to Penric.

Ree overcame intense self-consciousness of his stolen garments to offer, "This is my father's warehouse. Ser Ripol Richelon. I'm his son Ree. This man is Aulie Merin, and he's a thief. Among other things."

And if the watchmen construed that the trio had interrupted a robbery in progress, so much the better. Still unable to rise, Merin clutched at his throat and leaked constricted rasps, like a bladder deflating.

"He's bleeding," Sword-man noted of Merin. "Why can't he talk?" Not kneeling to help yet; he kept his eye on Penric.

"Sorcery," said Penric, truthfully. "Which is also why he can't walk right now. I did mention he just tried to knife me. You'll have to fetch a couple of bearers. He'll recover on his own in a while. Take him to whatever you use for a lockup, and keep him there till someone comes from the Temple or the city tomorrow to make it all official." The legal part of this mess should now fall into the hands of authorities who were *not Penric*, so that was a bright spot. Though there would doubtless be testimony required of him later. In writing.

"When he gets his voice back," said Ree bitterly, "I promise he'll use it to lie."

"Folks always do, to us," said Lantern-man. His gimlet gaze around did not specify who, except that it was likely those who were talking. If the watchmen arrested the wrong parties by mistake, would Learned Iserne come to free them?

She's a property lawyer, Pen.

I'll bet she knows people.

I'll bet she does too.

Pen moved this along in the hopes that assuming his conclusions would overbear further delays. "It's very late, and I have yet to escort the victim to his home and the saint back to the chapterhouse of our Order." And what Riesta would have to say about their dawn return Pen didn't dare guess. "We also need a guard placed on the door till its owner can come arrange repairs. May we leave this in your capable hands?"

Good flattery there, said Des. *Now follow up and bless the crap out of them.*

Pen did so, but thought unshipping his purse and paying in advance for the guard, and a few other details he didn't inquire into too deeply, did more. When he finished he didn't have enough left for boat fare back to the Isle of Gulls.

Borrow it from Iserne, Des suggested. *I imagine she'll be good for it.*

Though by now, he'd have emptied out every last coin just to get Merin safely into a cell. Vastly more efficient and less trouble than, say, chasing the fugitive through Lodi till he pitched into a canal and drowned from the weight of his stolen money belt.

Less satisfying, though, said Des. *Have I mentioned I actually like your overactive imagination?*

Speak for yourself. Bloody-minded demon. Yet the vivid picture of having to pull the rotting bodies of Chio and Ree out of some similar canal, had Merin had his way, drained Pen's thought of ire. Lodi canals were a deal warmer and less preserving than the chill Martensbridge lake.

The watchmen still squinted at them all, but the prospect of transferring the entire mess to the hands of the day shift probably did more to sway them than had Pen's coins and Learned Iserne's name and direction combined. They divided their tasks, one standing sentry and the other trotting off for reinforcements, and Pen seized the chance to slip his party away before yet more questioners arrived and he'd have to go over it all *again*.

Ree's dismasted leg was still not working right, so Pen heaved him up with his arm over his shoulder. He choked down a whimper.

Pen tried to herd the saint ahead of them to the ruined door, but at the last moment she darted back and searched out an ornamented hair stick from where it had rolled into a bale. Setting her teeth, she then bent, wrapped her fist around the glass ball of the one still in Merin's arm, and yanked it back out. Blood spattered on the wooden floor as he jerked and whined. Efficiently, she wiped the wet shank on his gray jacket.

Rejoining Pen and Ree, she wound her messy braid back up on her head and pinned it crookedly in place. Ree watched this firm gesture with, apparently, great admiration.

"Good," she said, collecting Merin's walking-lantern as well. "Let's go."

I'm not in charge of this parade anymore, am I, Des, Pen thought as they limped after the girl.

You haven't been all night. God-touched, if you didn't notice. I did.

...Aye.

IT WAS the deadest hour of the night. Even the most determined celebrants had staggered home, and early workers were not yet abroad. The lantern, held aloft by Chio as Pen supported Ree, guttered out of oil before they reached Iserne's house. The moon served, just high enough for its pale light to angle down between the close buildings.

Chio glanced over her shoulder. "Your whites make you glow like a ghost."

"Ghosts are grayer, usually."

"Oh? Not the ones I see."

"Maybe the god gets them fresher?"

Ree's brow wrinkled at this exchange.

As they made the last turn, Pen could see a single light still burning on the street, suspended from its chain over Iserne's door. This was one lamp that wasn't going to be allowed to run out of oil before dawn, he wagered.

"Up we go," he told Ree as they reached the steps, preparing to hoist, but Ree got more power out of his one working leg than Pen expected. His intent face lifted; Pen could feel his body shaking from more than just painful effort.

Rapid footfalls sounded from inside even as Pen raised his hand to the lion-faced doorknocker. He stepped back hastily before his second tap lest they be bumped back down the steps as the door was flung wide.

"*Ohfivegodsbethankedyou'resafe!*" Pen staggered a bit as Iserne fell on them, or rather on Ree. For a moment, she seemed to have four or six arms, not two, as she alternated between hugging her son, and inspecting him for injuries.

Chio's smile, as she watched this from the side, was secret, tender, and deeply pleased.

"What's wrong with your right arm?" Iserne demanded, taking up Ree's limp hand. She drew back only a little when she finally thought to ask Pen, "Is he all right now?"

Pen didn't think even the wild demon could have impeded this welcome-home. "Yes, thanks to Blessed Chio and our god, he's all himself again."

Iserne exhaled in vast relief.

"I'm afraid the numbness in his arm and his leg is the doing of my sorcery, but we had to hold"—he probably shouldn't use the nickname *Madboy* in front of Ree's mother—"the demon down for the saint to do her work, and it was, of course, resisting us."

"But—what—but come in, come in, all of you." She drew them into her hallway, casting a last look into the darkness. "Is Ser Merin not with you?"

"Not anymore," said Pen. "Long story, which we'll get to in a bit."

"Oh. Good." She shut the door firmly and shot the bolt. Turning back to them, she said to Ree, "Should you lie down? Should I send for a physician? I made you food."

"Learned Penric has some skills as a physician," Chio put in. "I don't think we need another tonight."

Yes, and how much did she know about that? Another private aspect of himself Pen knew he had not discussed. "Ree's few days at the Gift of the Sea helped the worst of his exposure and exhaustion. He could hardly have been delivered into more expert hands for that. The numbness should pass off in a while." Duration prudently unspecified.

"Yes, but what exactly did you *do* to him?" Iserne's scowl was more puzzled than angry, fortunately.

"Let's just say that learning sorcerous healing also teaches everything one could want to know about sorcerous hurting," said Pen. "Two sides of one coin." Which was why sorcerer-physicians were the rarest and most closely overseen of Temple servants. Pen was relieved when Iserne did not follow up with more questions, dismissing Pen and his late craft in favor of her more immediate concerns.

"Food would be good," said Ree. "And sitting. Then lie down. I'm so tired. But oh, Mother, I have so much to tell you. It was all such madness, and I'm still reeling." In truth, as he hung on his rescuer's shoulder, but only the physical part of that was Pen's doing. "Is Father back yet?"

"Not till next week, but I may hurry him with a note."

"Good. There are things he'll need to know, and Uncle Nigus, too."

"I have a meal laid out in the dining room. Please join us, Learned, Blessed." Her attempt to curtsey and beckon them on simultaneously resulted in a sort of hand-waving bob. Pen helped the halting Ree through the indicated archway off the entry hall—his left leg was getting more movement now, good. Chio set the spent lantern and their masks on a side table and followed.

Iserne had not been jesting. Enough fare for ten people was scattered across the Richelon family's dining table. The array was very miscellaneous, everything an invading army of one woman could possibly forage from a kitchen after midnight when she could not rest: ends of cold meat, cheeses, fruit and dried fruit, boiled eggs, cabbage salad, nuts, fresh-baked bread and cakes, custards, jam tarts, restoring herb tea, wines and water.

"So much food," muttered Pen. "How many people was she expecting?"

"I believe it was a prayer," Chio murmured from his other side.

Aye, Des agreed.

As Pen helped Ree into a chair, Iserne scurried to fetch a hand basin and towel, which, along with a sliver of fine white soap, she presented first to Chio, then Pen, then her son. Chio, who'd seated herself on Ree's right, helped his half-working hands with the washup.

Ree lifted his good hand toward the darkening bruise on her cheek. "Did I do that? I'm so sorry, Blessed Chio."

She didn't flinch. Shrugging off his apology, she said, "I know it wasn't really you. Anyway, it was Merin's fault for shoving me at you like that. He should have been praying, not cursing."

Iserne seized the chair on Ree's other side, leaving Pen to take the place across. "What's this tale?"

Ree's and Chio's tumbling joint account of the confrontation in the warehouse was understandably both garbled and horrifying, Ree's part not least because, famished, he kept trying to talk with his mouth full. Clarity was not much improved by them working backward, leapfrog fashion, from each of their vantages through the chaotic events of the evening leading up to it. Pen judged Ree was severely editing his hectic experiences spent under his ascendant demon for his mother's ears. He did awkwardly confess about the fellow he'd robbed for the clothing he still wore, drawing in Penric to give what he hoped were soothing reassurances.

"Wait," said Iserne, holding up her hands. "Go back to the beginning. You're saying *Merin* threw you from your ship? It wasn't an accident?"

Her teeth set as Ree disgorged a longer tale of his accusation of Merin and how it had come about, with a lot of names and details of merchant accounts and accounting that Pen did not follow but Iserne evidently did. It was clear Ree was regaining his wits, if not his composure.

"Embezzling. Well, I'm not surprised," she said.

"You're not? I was blindsided," said Ree.

"Plainly, someone should have told you, but Merin was your Uncle Nigus's man and problem, and so Ripol kept out of it. Nigus suspected sticky fingers back when Merin worked for him, but the losses all had other explanations—sly, I gathered—so he didn't think he could prove it in a law court. He solved his problem by recommending Merin on to one of his more bitter rivals. Which I thought as nearly dubious as the original thefts, but I wasn't consulted."

"I'd wondered why you didn't like him flattering Lonniel. I'd thought it was because he was too poor."

She sniffed. "Ripol was that poor when we first married. And a difficult time we had of it, but he met our challenges by working harder. Not by wasting all his cleverness taking dishonest shortcuts." She went on more intently, "But what happened *after* you were thrown into the water?"

Ree looked away, the fatigue underlying his sunburned features growing more marked. "I was so angry, I didn't even think to be frightened at first, till my cries went unheard and the ship sailed out of sight. I could guess which way was east by the moon, as long as it was above the horizon, and by the stars a little. And the sun when dawn came. I didn't think I could make it, but I swam toward the coast as best I could. Slower and slower as I grew tired. Finally it was all I could do to stay afloat. I thought, well, I thought about a lot of things. Things I should have done, and shouldn't have, and all the things I was never going to get to do."

Iserne's hand pressed her lips, and she didn't interrupt. Chio listened with grave interest, head bent toward him.

"The dolphin was the strangest part," Ree went on, "coming up under me in the dawn just when I couldn't swim anymore. I'd never been so close to one before, let alone touched it. Its skin was all slick, cool and firm like wet leather. Except lumpy—I think now the bumps must have been tumors, because some were broken open and infected, and there was a memory of pain, later. Not easy to hang onto, but I swear it waited for me like a good horse. We must have moved slowly toward Adria all that long day. Then it died, and sank from under me, and I thought I had gone mad from fear at last. I can scarcely remember the fishermen, I was so confused by then. We should find them to thank them."

"Oh yes," said Iserne fervently.

"The people from the hospice may be able to identify them for you," Pen suggested. "If someone takes back that concussed fellow's clothes and purse, you could ask then. He's owed thanks of a sort, too, I think."

"Does he know what he owes to you?" Chio asked Pen in curiosity.

All right, it could have been his life, if the rats had been quicker and hungrier, or if Madboy had bashed him harder. Pen waved this away. "He owes me nothing. All in a Bastard's Eve work." Pen's holiday, hah.

Ree looked perturbed at this reminder, and altogether too grateful to his mother when she said, "I'll take on that task tomorrow."

"You're likely the person best suited to make sure there are no repercussions," Pen agreed. "There's going to be enough of a legal tangle with Merin." Pen was glad his Temple duties ended with the demon and the saint, the machineries of justice being the prerogative of the city and a very different god than his own.

A feminine voice, sleepy and miffed, sounded from the archway. "You're having a feast? And you didn't wake me up?" Then a gasp. "*Ree!*"

Pen looked up, and Ree twisted around in his chair, to see Lonniel pick up the skirts of her night-dress and pelt the few steps to her brother's side. Iserne had to lean away as she grabbed him in an excited hug and ran her anxious fingers through his hair in a sisterly echo of his mother's earlier greeting. "How is your head?"

"My head? Much better than it was, now I'm alone in it again."

"It's not broken after all?" she said as her searching fingers found neither lumps nor clotted blood.

"No, that was the other fellow, but Learned Penric says he'll get better."

"What?" They blinked at each other in mirrored confusion.

Penric explained to Ree, "We stopped here earlier, after we first encountered Iserne and Merin searching for you in the hospice. Merin didn't want to mention your near-drowning or the demon, which he'd just found out about himself—Bastard's teeth, that must have come as a shock. Nor tell the truth, for obvious reasons. So he told your sisters that after your ship moored in Lodi you'd run off due to being hit on the head in an unloading accident."

"Son of a bitch," growled Ree. "Whyever did he come here in the first place?"

"To bring the news to your mother of your loss overboard sailing up to the last stop in Trigonie," said Chio. "He claimed he was sent to do so, on account of you two being cabinmates and him knowing your family, but I'll bet he volunteered, to make sure only the right things were said."

Ree's jaw dropped at this outrageousness, echoed by Iserne's affronted huff.

Chio mused on, "You have to admire his nerve, in a way. To face his murder victim's mother and tell all those smooth lies. I knew he was sweating about it, but I didn't realize why."

"*What?*" shrieked Lonniel.

Her mother, not willing to give up her place, sent her around the table to sit next to Penric as Ree began his tale once more. Wide-eyed, she worked her way through two fruit tarts and a pile of pistachios as he brought his synopsis up from his fall into the sea to the mortal fight in their father's warehouse.

He paused and cleared his throat. "If you were sweet on Merin, I'm sorry."

She made a wry face. "Not especially? He made sheep's-eyes at me, but so do the other young fellows who work for Father and Uncle. I knew he was angry and resentful of anyone with more luck than himself, which to hear him tell it seemed to be most people. I never dreamed he'd take it so far."

"To be fair," said Pen, seminary debate-habits lingering, "I don't think he'd ever planned murder. His main aim seemed to be theft. But when Ree caught him out, things went from bad to worse, each rash impulse struggling to fix the one before it." Pen contemplated this. "Ending with trying to *stab a saint*, which strikes me as epically stupid." He frowned at Chio. "Though the god could not have protected you from a blade, you know."

Her lips curved up. "Of course He could. He sent you."

Pen buried his flattered, horrified grumble in a bite of fig.

"Saint…?" said Lonniel faintly, stopping in mid-chew.

"I was just getting to that part," said Ree, his tired face growing eager as he glanced over at Chio. "It's how the Temple gets rid of demons, you know. Or maybe you don't. I can't say as I really knew, before, just a dim notion that someone from the white god's Order took care of such things."

"That someone would be me, for the archdivineship of Lodi," Chio said, with a tentative smile across the table at Lonniel.

"Uh, had we introduced Blessed Chio to you when we met earlier?" asked Penric. He couldn't remember, in the welter of subsequent events.

"*Blessed* Chio…?" Lonniel shook her head. "No! Nor you either, properly, Learned," she added as an afterthought. "A real sorcerer, come to our house? Nobody tells me *anything* important."

Iserne bit her lip, possibly on a tart reminder that they'd caught the sisters sneaking out the door, not an incident to invite much in the way of confidences.

"My apologies," Pen interjected, before Iserne was pricked into saying anything that might restart some chronic mother-daughter dispute. "Penric kin Jurald, court sorcerer to Archdivine Ogial. And Blessed Chio, my Order's saint residing at the chapterhouse of the Isle of Gulls. I was originally sent by the archdivine to look into the case of the shiplost man brought to the Gift of the Sea, and, well, we have." He gestured at Ree, and by extension at the whole tumultuous night.

Lonniel, her brows scrunching, asked her brother, "What was it like? Having a demon?" An eye-flick at Pen, as she realized another demon must be sitting next to her. She didn't, quite, edge away.

Ree made a helpless hand-wave. "A horrible fever dream, that went on and on and I couldn't wake up from it. Memories that weren't mine, running through my head. Some terrible—strangling and being strangled all atop, gods that Roknari man was more awful than Merin—some just strange.

Moving through the water, weightless and joyful
and powerful. Crunching down all those wriggling
live fish, ugh. My body walking around Lodi on
its own, and I could only watch as it did things I
didn't choose. I got all the bruises and hunger just
the same. When the god came and took it away...I
can't..." His voice died.

Chio, listening, smiled quietly at that.

He shifted to face her. "You do this over and
over? The god comes to you each time?"

She tilted her head. "Whenever the Order brings
me another elemental. It's an unsteady supply, but
maybe four to six a year."

"It—that experience—must...do things. To
you." As it just had to Ree?

She considered this in kindly seriousness. "The
god...enlarges my world?"

Or her soul, Pen suspected. And she confronted
this vastness six times a year? One direct encounter—two, now—with his god in Pen's lifetime had
been overwhelming enough.

"How can you bear it? That demon was so
dreadful."

"That one was very, very bad," she agreed with a
sigh. "With new elementals, caught early, it's more

like killing chickens. Uncanny chickens, but still. An unpleasant task I try to make as mercifully quick as possible."

Which meant the one in the warehouse had felt more like hanging a human? Chio did not point this up, so neither did Pen.

"Will you always be a saint?" asked Ree.

"I'm at the god's disposal, not Him at mine. Any time could be the last, I expect."

Pen offered, "I believe the Saint of Idau has served the region around Martensbridge for over thirty years. He's quite aged now, but he's still at it as far as I know." Blessed Broylin's calling must have come upon him in mid-life, Pen realized. That had to be a story, and he regretted not collecting it. But, indeed, sorcerers did not linger around saints to socialize.

Lonniel asked, "Will the Bastard's Order always keep you on the Isle of Gulls? Like...like a princess in a tower?"

A more gratifying comparison than *a prisoner in a dungeon*, Pen supposed.

Chio was surprised into a laugh. "I'm sure Learned Riesta—my chapterhouse supervisor— wishes he could. But I'm devotee to the Bastard, not to the Daughter of Spring. I have no religious duty to withdraw from the world. I can have whatever life I can arrange. You said Broylin was a baker, Penric? I wonder whatever happened to that dressmaker... Now I'm not a child, I stay on Gulls mainly because I can't afford to take myself elsewhere." She grew thoughtful. "Does Riesta keep me poor on purpose for that?"

"I could not speculate," said Pen, deciding to be diplomatic.

"Maybe it's just his frugal habit," she said, tolerantly. "The orphanage always has too many mouths to feed."

"Can saints marry?" asked Lonniel. Pen approved her avid curiosity, if not her bluntness.

Iserne, alive to the hazards of both, and perhaps to spare Chio awkwardness, answered this one. "I've met two petty saints, judges in the Father's Order, who are married. To each other, which must make for peculiar bed-talk. And one saint-acolyte in the Mother's, whom I encountered when I helped draw up her will some years ago. So yes. About as commonly as other people, I imagine."

"Oh. I was wondering, because of the Bastard's Order. That maybe it wasn't done over there, on account of some, um, courtesy to the god."

"Yes, people in our Order do marry." Penric cleared his throat. "Sorcerers maybe less often. I'm given to understand our demons make us difficult as spouses. Five of Desdemona's—that is, my demon's—prior riders managed somehow, though. All of them were wed before they became sorceresses, come to think. But never two mages to each other. Two chaos demons in one household would be, how to put this, an oversupply of chaos in one place." Or even two chaos demons in one palace, which was how he came to be booted out of Martensbridge.

"What about a sorcerer and a saint?" Lonniel went on, irrepressibly. Pen estimated she was of the age when marriage loomed as her next great life passage, hence this alarming focus.

Her mother rolled her eyes, reproving, "Lonniel."

"No," Des answered aloud firmly, before Pen could speak again.

"Oh. Too bad." Her gaze flicked at her brother as she continued to serenely demolish her pear.

So may a sorcerer and a saint be friends?

Across a table seems all right, Des allowed, sounding bemused at the discovery. *In the same bed would be much too close.*

Well, quite.

"So…you would be, um, allowed visitors, Blessed Chio?" said Ree in a tentative tone. "At your chapterhouse?"

Chio lifted one slim shoulder. "If any ever came out to Gulls." She added to Lonniel, "We don't actually have any towers at the orphanage. It might be fun to live in one, if not as a prisoner. There'd be a handsome view of the basin, and the city. Much better than the girls' dormitory, though they gave me my own room in the chapterhouse after my calling came upon me. They needed the dormer bed for the next orphan, I expect."

Lonniel's eyes brightened, and she gestured urgently with her pear core. "Could we come? And visit you?"

Ree's startled glance shifted to his sister. "What a, a good idea."

Des, watching the play, started to silently laugh. *Well, there's a sister who's just earned herself some brotherly love.*

What?

Do keep up, Pen.

Iserne said judiciously, "We could all go out. Ripol will certainly want to meet and thank Blessed Chio, when he returns."

Lonniel perked up at this offered treat. Ree cast his mother a grateful look.

Is Iserne keeping up, too?

Oh, I think so.

Iserne bestowed a benign smile upon the saint. Upon the unmarried young woman? Both?

"Be warned," said Chio, "Learned Riesta will ask you for donations to the orphanage. He always does, no matter who comes. From the archdivine down to the boatmen."

"Then we'll be in good company," said Iserne, undeterred.

Lonniel bounced in her chair. "Ooh, yes, let's all make a day of it when Papa gets back."

"You'd be very welcome," said Chio. Her expression warmed as it dawned on her that Iserne's offer was not just a social fib, made to be polite and as lightly forgotten, but a real promise. "All of you."

In the tug between admiring Chio, and falling face-first into his plate, Ree's plate was starting to win. They'd all eaten till they couldn't hold more, both Lonniel and Chio demonstrating impressive capacities. What food was left on the table would have to fend for itself, Pen thought muzzily. Ree wasn't the only one for whom the horizontal beckoned. A gray light leaked through the dining chamber's shutters, harbinger of the early midsummer dawn.

"I should escort Blessed Chio back to Gulls," Pen announced to the air generally. And wasn't that going to be awkward at this late hour. He briefly pictured dropping the disheveled girl off at the chapterhouse boat landing like a package and fleeing back across the water, but no, that would be cowardly. The saint had set a daunting example of courage and nerve tonight, so Pen needed to hold up the honor of, of...sorcerers, or whatever. *For the Order and the White God!* he imagined declaiming, except that he was fairly certain his god would just laugh at him.

"Oh. Yes, of course." Iserne, too, had to pull herself away from a fascinated study of her young guest. "It's so late it's become early." Her expression softened at her son. "Ree should go to bed, before he needs carrying up in a sack. I can't do that any-more, now he's man-sized."

Ree made a grunt of exhausted agreement, but pulled himself together as Pen and Chio rose. He managed to stand, holding the back of his chair, and offered her a precarious bow. "Blessed Chio. I hope to see you again soon."

She touched her forehead, mouth, navel, groin, and heart in the tally of five-fold benediction, tapped the back of her thumb to her lips, and pressed it to his forehead. "The white god guard you until then."

"He has been. Hasn't He? You would know."

A secret smile, but it might be a secret shared with Ree. "Maybe."

Pen trailed after her into the entryway, like a pilot boat to some homegoing sailing vessel. There followed the confusions of departure, Pen in embarrassment begging Iserne for oarboat fare, his mumbled apologies overborne by her grateful generosity of coins. He could catch up to her next week in the curia and pay her back, he consoled himself.

Iserne gave them careful directions to the nearest public landing at the mouth of the Wealdmen's Canal, where Pen hoped they would find some early, or late, boatman waiting for work. He considered, for about two seconds, saving money by walking, again, all across town to the landing closer to Gulls on the city basin. *No.* The Richelon door closed on the happy fuss of his mother and sister getting Ree aimed up the stairs to his bed, and his unconvincing protests of self-sufficiency.

THE RISING light was turning the misty shore air to silver as they arrived at the landing, where they found a sleepy and thankfully ungarrulous boatman waiting to start his busy Bastard's Day labors. Pen settled Chio in the forward-facing seat and took the one across from her. The boatman shoved them off with a surge that settled into gentle and soporific rocking.

Pen blinked gritty eyes, and remembered: "Oh. Happy birthday, Blessed Chio. Will you at least get sweet custard, later?"

"I trust so. The chapterhouse does put on a fine Bastard's Day feast, once we have endured Riesta's homilies. The orphans work up good appetites during the afternoon games in the god's honor. Though right now I'm too full to care." She tilted her head back to the warming sky. "Learned Iserne is a generous mother. I wonder if Ree, and Lonniel, and Lepia know how lucky they are."

And Ripol, presumably. Not hard to see who was the strong glue holding that household together.

"They seem an admirable family," Chio went on. "Much the sort I once dreamed of being adopted into. I'm too old for that now." That telling I-don't-care one-shoulder shrug, again.

"It's a family at a late stage," Pen observed idly. "You're seeing the results of many years of labors, not the labor itself. I grew up in a largish family myself, but as the lastborn, I never saw the beginnings either. We children mostly couldn't wait to get away, toward the end." Pen's older brother Drovo, disastrously into a mercenary company. His sisters more naturally passing into marriage, nothing fatal there, yet. The eldest Rolsch stuck forever at the core, though as baron he presumably had compensations pleasing to him. Penric...well. He'd always been the odd duck.

Swan, by now, suggested Des. *Look, you're even garbed in white feathers.*

Seriously smudged and ruffled, after the past night. White was a terrible choice of emblematic color for a god of chaos.

Reminded of his sisters, it occurred to Pen there was another way for a young woman to acquire a family, very traditional indeed. But surely merchant clans did not approve portionless brides? The richer orphanages did sometimes bestow modest dowries upon their girls, he'd heard, though more often the houses were pressed just to come up with appren-ticeship fees. It might be unkind to put such a notion into Chio's head.

He offered instead, "The princess-archdivine once quipped to me that our friends are what the gods give us to make up for our families." In one of their more wine-mellowed late-night chats—though he suspected the hallow kings of the Weald experienced family on a whole different level.

Not that different, said Des, and how did she know?

Chio, at least, smiled at Pen's imported joke.

Her orphan state wasn't a problem he could fix by any sorcery of his. That was a task for their god's hand, perhaps. Though one needed to be *cautious* in prayers to the Bastard.

Oh, come, Des scoffed. *What makes you think His hand wasn't stirring this pot all night? And possibly before then. I don't think you need to say a word.*

Parsimony, or opportunism? Why not both...?

I'd bet on Ree, myself. Young. Energetic. Grateful...

There's no tower to rescue this princess from, Pen pointed out.

The lad seems resourceful. He might build one just to rescue her from it.

Hah.

Pen wished Chio well in any case. Whatever that *well* turned out to be.

Chio sat up and pointed out across the glinting waters. "Ooh, look! The boats are starting to come in for the Bastard's Day procession."

Pen followed her line. Either a big oarboat or a small galley, five oars on a side, sculled along overtaking them. It was painted, or freshly repainted, in white, with scrolling decorations of silver or more likely tin feigning silver, festooned with garlands and flowers, pennants flirting with the air.

"That's the boat from the Glass Island chapterhouse," Chio identified it. She waved wildly at its occupants, who waved back. A grinning woman at the rail, taking in Pen's vestments, tossed them a shouted blessing and a circlet of white flowers, which fell short and landed in the water. Chio made their boatman swerve aside. Pen grabbed the thwart as their boat wobbled when she leaned over to pluck it out and shake it off. She plopped it atop her head, where it sat askew.

"Are there orphan boats from Glass Island, too?" Pen asked, looking around for such. The decorated flotilla of small vessels following the chapterhouse craft seemed to be a miscellaneous lot, but children were only thinly scattered among their passengers.

"No, Glass doesn't have an orphanage."

"I never thought to ask. Are you supposed to be in the procession today?" As an honored saint now, not displayed as hopeful human wares. If so, Pen was going to be delivering her late for it, oops.

"Mm, no, the five Orders here tend to keep all their saints very private. The Father's and the Mother's people, I know, so that they won't get pestered to distraction by supplicants. My task is too specialized to draw supplicants, except those who *really* need me. Who are generally guided in." Her grin flickered. "Like you."

Pen wasn't sure but what *blundered* might be a better term than *guided*, for his Bastard's Eve.

"You have fine weather for the procession, this morning," Pen allowed. The lagoon's soft air felt good on his face, though by noon they'd all be seeking shade.

"It's usually so at midsummer," the boatman put in, the first he'd interrupted—though he had been, inescapably, listening. Slow to wake up, maybe; Pen sympathized. But everyone was allowed to comment on the weather, everywhere, as far as Pen had observed. "Sometimes there's wind. The equinoxes are more chancy. I row for the Father's procession at winter solstice. Chilly, and properly somber if there's mist. Your hands get chapped." He nodded and, evidently satisfied to have said his piece, went back to his rhythmic sweeping.

Five gods, five major festivals; the Bastard's Day always taking over Mother's Midsummer in Quintarian lands. The three other holy days that fell exactly between the solstices and equinoxes found alternate excuses for their celebrations.

The Quadrenes tuck our god's intercalary day in at Father's Midwinter, Des remarked, *because they imagine it keeps Him under better control. It's considered a day of ill luck, for fasting and prayer, where no one goes out or starts any new enterprise.* A pause for consideration, or perhaps memory, for she added, *Young Umelan always found it very boring.*

Pen squinted and yawned. The boatman likely wouldn't be too startled if his passenger curled up on the bottom of his boat and started snoring. He had to have ferried home plenty of exhausted holiday-goers over the years, if none quite this late, nor from a night this strange.

Chio had fallen silent, studying the shifting cityscape as they reached the central basin. Fatigue seemed to be gaining on her at last, though not as much as on Pen. He didn't often meet anyone who made him feel quite so old.

The sense of a snort from Des, which he prudently ignored.

It occurred to Pen, watching Chio trail a meditative hand in the water, that there was one aspect of her night's saintly labors she had entirely talked around at the Richelons' table. And that his duty to her as a divine of their shared Order extended beyond merely acting as her guardsman. Even if she'd handed him back as much defending as he'd given to her, which was a trifle embarrassing.

She has the god's guidance, Pen. Why would she need yours?

Cogent question, but... *Let's find out.*

It took him a moment or two to decide how to start.

"When I was nineteen, and feckless, and knew almost nothing yet about my new calling as a sorcerer, it never even crossed my mind to wonder what distress disposing of Des would have caused old Broylin. He was presented to me as already an authority, an immovable fixture in the world, like a mountain. He seemed surprised when the god refused my demon, but not...not unhappy. I just assumed he'd seen many and worse. I know of one for certain—a renegade Temple demon, which must have become a full person by the time it was recalled and destroyed by the god." Des's memories of Tigney's ascendant demon were fraught enough, shared only reluctantly with Pen.

Chio shook the droplets off her hand and turned toward him. "You're a noticing sort of man, Learned Penric. In ways Riesta can't be, I guess."

Pen opened a conceding palm. "Yes."

A little silence. Then, "In a way," Chio said, "I'm glad this one was such an awful mess. At least there wasn't doubt, atop the other ugliness of my task. If that was a birthday gift to me from the god, well...it's not as if I can give it back."

"Good is not always the same thing as nice, they say." He studied her tired young face in the light of the sun, now topping the city and piercing the watery silver air with rose-gold. It would be a fine fair day, and hot. "Are you going to be all right?"

"I...will be." She puffed a faint laugh, adding, "You're the first to ever ask me that, at one of these duties. Everyone asked it of that chicken-woman, after I freed her, but not of me. Not even me. Her elemental hadn't been in her long enough to pick up more than a trace of humanity. It was like erasing a shadow. This...wasn't like that. *Full person*, yes. Very full." Her eyes sought the passing shoreline. "The god grieved for the fate of His creature."

Did her hands feel stained with that fate? "It was seven lives deep, by my count, however short some were, and had grown dark and twisted. I don't think any other rider could have healed it by that stage. Not even by all our god's contriving."

"This, I saw." She turned back to him. "Your demon is much, much deeper, but not dark. She glows, like colored lanterns in a vast winding cavern."

Des had been seeing nothing in that moment of demon-destruction, like a child hiding its head under a blanket from night terrors. But if Chio had been watching over the white god's shoulder, nothing would have been hidden from her. It was probably well such moments were short, so that the gods could return their saints to the world still sane. Mostly.

Chio's curious look across at Pen grew grave, unblinking. "What do you grieve for so hard, Learned?"

Oh. So it wasn't just Des that she'd seen into, or Merin and Ree.

He shrugged in discomfort. "In time, most of us become orphans, it turns out. The princess-archdivine had been like a second mother to me. And as great a loss, last year." As that bereavement had fallen bare months before the death of his first mother, Pen supposed he had an exact-enough standard of comparison, though he wasn't sure such a balance-scale made any sense, really.

Chio rocked back, absorbing this. Then leaned forward. "That wasn't all, I think?"

Pen made a face, starting to pass this off as nothing more, nothing much. But Chio seemed not the person for lies this morning, neither as saint nor as young woman. Not when he'd just been demanding truths from her.

He took a breath, for resolution. "I had been working hard to make a new career as a Temple physician-sorcerer, to please all who had cared for me. It wasn't that I was not good at it. That would have made it so much easier to quit. Not a failure of skills, but of…character, perhaps." He averted Des's beginning fulmination with a hasty, "Or maybe just a mismatch between soul and calling. Serious mismatch. It broke something."

Your heart, I thought, said Des. Her dry tone robbed the comment of mawkishness. *And I was there. So don't try to tell me lies, either. It was your error in the first place, for imagining you had to save every patient brought before you. …Not that you didn't try.*

The failed physician, and the uncanny executioner… Chio, he thought, might understand that futile feeling of lives, and deaths, slipping through a grasp oddly well. *Oh.*

Pen rubbed at his forearms, nervously. "I really don't care to speak of it."

"I see that," said Chio. Her head tilted in a concentration upon him that Pen found unnerving. "…I believe your demon isn't the only creature our god wishes to keep in this world."

"This… I…already know. Received that message very clear. On a hillside above Martensbridge, one morning last fall. Which is why I never made it to my investiture ceremony in the Mother's Order that noon."

If you had succeeded *in cutting your bloody arms off,*
you'd have taken me with you, you know, Des grumped.
As I pointed out at the time, but you weren't listening to
much of anything by then. Certainly not reason.

Yes. I apologize. There won't be a repeat.

Best not be. The sense of a peeved *Harumph!*
concealing…much. Love, Pen suspected.

"And so I'm here," Pen concluded. Whether in
Lodi or the world he left unsaid.

"And so you are." A determined nod, as if Chio
might share her very considerable spine with him—
another birthday gift that could not be turned
down. "I'm glad of it."

At the mouth of the main canal, across the
basin, the holy procession was assembling. Chio
exclaimed, pointing out the archdivine's fancy
barge being brought out for the blessing: two
stacked rows of oarsmen, bunting and flags, the
tiny, glittering figures of prelates and functionaries all in their best finery. Sweet sounds from
musicians and a choir on an upper deck carried
clearly across the water. Pen wagered he could have
elbowed his way to a place aboard if he'd been over
there this morning, although by now he thought
he'd rather elbow into his bed. Gull Island's orphan

floats had presumably already rowed off to join in. He was so fascinated by the shining spectacle, he only turned around when the oarboat swung in for their landing.

Where he discovered that Iserne had not been the only parent up all night waiting for the return of a lost one. Learned Riesta, his back bowed and elbows propped on his knees, sat on the edge of the jetty with his legs dangling over, head nodding.

His face jerked up as their hull scraped against the stone. "Chio!" He scrambled to his feet to march down the water-stairs, hands reaching to help her out of the boat. Pen was left to fend for his own balance, not to mention pay the oarsman.

It was that last addition of the damp flower crown, listing drunkenly atop her head, that pushed Chio's appearance over the line from *disheveled* to *debauched*, Pen decided as he turned and climbed the steps to join them. And her muted grin. His own bleary, squinting eyes and numb face probably just looked wine-sick. In neither case a reassuring sight for an anxious guardian.

"Where have you two *been* all night?" Riesta demanded. His tone was more strangled than thundering.

"Oh, Learned Penric brought me the most splendid Bastard's Eve ever!" Chio told him cheerily. "We walked all over town to the market parties, ate festival food, tracked down the ascendant demon, rescued its rider, and captured a murderer. And I hear Learned Penric revived a robbery victim and reformed a cutpurse, though even the god wasn't entirely sure that last was going to stick." Her sly grin widened as she capped this with, "Also I met a very nice boy, together with his family."

Was she *teasing* the poor man? And not for the first time, judging by his exasperated sigh. "*Chio...*"

Pen was acquiring new insight into the relationship between the stodgy Temple functionary and his saint, to be sure. He might have to reclassify Riesta from *forbidding* to *beleaguered*. It was revealing that he didn't even bother to tax Penric on the alarming progression of the night's events. Nor to generate the sorts of wild accusations of him that a girl missing all night might be expected to foster in a paternal mind, which Pen had been braced to counter.

Nor did he offer the least hint that he deemed she could be lying to him, despite her provoking summary. Interesting...

Pen thought to add, "There will probably be a city magistrate's inquiry about the murderer, but not until tomorrow. If they want more than the saint's testimony, send them on to me at the curia."

Riesta did not look as if this news helped.

Chio patted Riesta's arm in a consolatory fashion. "I'll give you a proper report on the demon for the Order's files later, I promise. Right now I want a wash-up and a nap."

"Well," he said, testiness overborne, "Well, see you do..."

Penric walked beside them as they started up the path beside the access canal to the chapterhouse, feeling vaguely that as escort he was obliged to at least see the young lady to her door.

Riesta eyed him sideways. "You survived, I see."

He meant the question ironically, but Pen thought of how close Merin's knife had come. The nick on his arm had dried; the bloodstain on his sleeve could be treated later. He answered less ironically, "Barely. But it seems I had a good protector."

Chio smirked, fiddling with the feathered mask dangling from her hand.

"It was a miracle my whites avoided the canals all night," he added. Not that this had saved them—they would still require extensive laundry and repairs.

Chio made a moue, and stopped, the two men perforce with her. "You sound so disappointed, Learned Penric. Is there no one to uphold the reputation of Lodi and our lord of chaos? We should give the god an offering on His day. Hand me your mask."

Pen did so, confused. Or stupid with fatigue, whichever.

She turned him to face her, adjusting his stance. He was just opening his mouth to inquire her meaning when she placed both hands on his chest and gave him a vigorous shove. Over the cut-stone bank and into the waters, backward, with a vast splash. His surprised yelp cut off with a gargle.

Spluttering up through clinging weeds, he found his feet, to discover the water here was only chest-deep.

Des! Why didn't you defend us?

This has to be the cleanest canal we've passed all night. Besides, how is a mere demon to stand up to the will of a saint?

You feign demure *badly, you know.* Or else she was still smug over that *vast, lamplit cavern* compliment, and had switched sides.

Never, she promised him. *Are you awake now? Invigorated? Cheered up...?*

Pen looked up to find Chio's laughing face, and Riesta's resigned one, leaning over the bank. The hands that had pushed him in now extended to help him out. ...And wasn't that a fitting metaphor for their god.

Helplessly, he laughed back, and took them.